Also by [

MIDNIGHT HEAT
The Fake Boyfriend Fiasco
The Princess Trap
The Roommate Risk

THE BROWN SISTERS
Get a Life, Chloe Brown
Take a Hint, Dani Brown
Act Your Age, Eve Brown

RAVENSWOOD
A Girl Like Her
Damaged Goods
Untouchable
That Kind of Guy

STANDALONE TITLES
Work for It
Guarding Temptation
Merry Inkmas
Wrapped Up in You

FOR TEENS
Highly Suspicious and Unfairly Cute

THE FAKE BOYFRIEND FIASCO

TALIA HIBBERT

Cover and Jacket Art © Erin O'Neill Jones
Relaunch Edits: Jennifer Scarberry

Published by Nixon House
ISBN: 978-1-913651-09-1

www.nixonhouse.co.uk

For my reckless hero.

Content Note

The Fake Boyfriend Fiasco is a super-spicy, bonkers romance with a guaranteed happy ending.

However, this story contains elements that could trigger certain audiences, including:

- Discussions of stalking, attempted murder, and associated trauma.
- Depictions of counselling.
- Depictions of excessive alcohol use.
- Discussion of drugs.
- Biphobia (challenged on the page).

Please take care of yourself when reading.

A Dark and Foreboding
Prologue

December 2017

Dr. Browne leant back in his seat, pen and notepad at the ready. "Perhaps we might discuss what happened in November?"

Aria Granger shrugged and looked around the room, stalling. Putting off the inevitable moment when she'd blurt everything out in embarrassing detail. She usually didn't have trouble keeping her mouth shut—far from it—but therapy was really loosening her up.

She didn't like it at all.

Her gaze settled on the desk to her left, a few metres away from the cozy sitting area they currently occupied. The sofa she sat on was squishy and plush and welcoming as hell, but the desk was all business. Browne had one of those odd ornaments that moved; a row of metal balls hanging from a frame, where one ball would swing into the next, and so on. Fancy having a thing like that. She'd only ever seen them on TV.

"Aria?" he prompted gently. He was being very... not *quiet*, but soft. As if she was a nervous pet: tame, but currently unsettled. He was careful not to scare her, confident that she'd come to him soon.

1

"November," she said slowly, if only to stop him talking. She couldn't bear that tone in a man's voice. "November... well. I finally got a tattoo on my shin. I'd been thinking about it for ages, and I'm running out of space for big pieces. But the idea of a needle on my *shin*—it proper set me wrong. Know what I mean? Shins are funny things, aren't they? I don't even like touching my own shins. Goes right through me."

He watched her with the appearance of patience. She felt slightly guilty. She'd told Jenny she'd take this seriously—and Theo, bless his heart, was paying by the hour. Not that he couldn't afford it, but still.

"I managed, in the end," she said. "My boss did it for me, Tara. She's got a light touch, so it wasn't that bad. Wasn't good, but it wasn't *bad*. That's usually the way, isn't it? You build things up in your mind, and then everything turns out fine."

Dr. Browne scrawled a few words onto his notepad. Or maybe it was a few sentences. Maybe he'd scribbled down the hook to *Independent Women*—she had no idea, because she couldn't read upside down and even if she could, his handwriting was an absolute state.

What could he have to say right now, anyway? *Client is a dizzy cow*? Or maybe, *Client thinks she's slick but I'm on to her*. She was probably better off not knowing. Curiosity killed the cat and all that. Only, she found it hard to leave things unknown, these days. Really hard. Unanswered questions made her itch. And that wasn't healthy at all, now was it?

With a sigh, Aria started again. "In November, my best friend was kidnapped."

He nodded. Maybe he already knew. Was Jen seeing this guy too? Or would that be unethical—like, a conflict, or a confidentiality issue, or something? She had no idea. She'd Google it.

"Tell me about that," he prompted.

Talk about opening a can of worms. "Alright. I had this

boyfriend—Simon. He was okay. He met Jen a few times—she was my roommate, you see. We're like sisters, have been forever. Anyway, it's a long story but... he'd been stalking her for a while, and he got with me for greater access to her. I had no idea, like none—I mean, obviously, but you know. Wow. I was fucking oblivious. So eventually, he goes right off the deep end and kidnaps her. There was a big police stand-off and everything, I was there. He was going to kill her. He held a gun to her head."

Dr. Browne offered Aria a wad of tissues, his moustache quivering sympathetically. She accepted them slowly, because she was confused. Then she noticed the hot trickle of tears rolling down her cheek. Oh, dear. Her eyeliner was probably done for.

She patted at her eyes awkwardly. What she really wanted to do was blow her nose, hard, but it would be all snotty and messy and she'd need a thousand more tissues. Nose blowing was one of those things that didn't mean much but felt oddly private. She willed the snot to dry up on its own.

"So, everything turned out kind of alright—I mean, Jen's fine and Simon's..." she swallowed. "Dealt with. Or whatever. Everyone's back to normal. Actually, Jen's great. She's engaged, isn't that fabulous? I'm planning the wedding. It's quite soon. I'm rushed off my feet, to be honest. I've never planned a wedding before, but if I left it to her she'd turn up at the registry office in an ivory pinafore or some such nonsense. She doesn't like a fuss. But I think she deserves a fuss."

"I see. Quite a whirlwind, isn't it?"

"Yeah, but I think they're really in love."

"Oh, no," Dr. Browne said. "I meant the kidnapping and associated events. It must have come as a huge shock. For someone you cared about, this Simon, to— "

Aria couldn't let the good doctor finish a sentence like that, because she might come over all anxious. Or furious. Or nauseous. Difficult to predict, these days. Best to cut off this line of inquiry completely.

"It wasn't that serious," she said. Her voice was just right: calm, almost blasé. "I was upset about Jenny, obviously, but I didn't give a fu—sorry. I didn't care about Simon, not like that."

Dr. Browne looked calm and blank, which meant he didn't believe her at all. "I understand. But for an intimate relationship to end in such a manner..."

"It's not like I was in love with him or anything," she said quickly. Which wasn't strictly true—in fact, it wasn't true at all.

But Aria was starting to think her love didn't mean much, anyway.

Chapter 1

Scouting for Boys

Three Months Later

"Aren't you a *vision*," Keynes drawled. "Skulking in the shadows, admiring your handiwork."

Aria narrowed her eyes as the best man wandered off the dance floor toward her. His suit jacket was nowhere to be seen, his bow-tie hung loose around his neck, and his shirt sleeves were rolled up to reveal caramel skin dusted with tawny hair. He was grinning, and gorgeous enough to make a (vain) girl jealous.

"Fuck off," she said.

He came to lean against the cool marble pillar beside her. "You first. Got a light?"

"Nope."

"Doesn't matter; I have. Got a cig?" The slang sounded preposterous in his private-schoolboy accent, but she'd gotten used to Keynes over the months since they'd first met. In fact, if this were primary school, he'd be her second-best friend by now.

Still, she glowered at him. "You're interrupting my brooding."

"That's the idea, love. Got a cig, or not?"

"You know I have."

"Yep." He produced a lighter from his pocket—a sickeningly slick little thing, silver and gold. No common-or-garden plastic Bic for Mr. Olusegun-Keynes.

With a sigh, Aria hiked up the gauzy skirt of her sunshine-yellow gown.

Keynes averted his eyes with all the drama of a stage dame. "Behave yourself, madam. You know I'm immune to your wiles."

"More's the pity," she muttered, snatching a cigarette from her garter. "I've only got one. We'll have to share."

"One, because?"

"Because your sister scared me into almost-quitting, and I'm trying to be good."

"Don't listen to her." Keynes lit the cigarette as Aria held it to her lips. "She's all talk. Once she's had a few drinks—"

"Stop enabling. I should quit, and so should you."

He plucked the cigarette from her fingers and took a drag. Then he said, smoke trailing from his full lips like dragon's breath, "I *have* quit, love. But enough about me. What are you doing over here?"

Excellent question. Aria was usually the life and soul of any party—and this wasn't just a party. It was her best friend's luxurious wedding at a fancy Greek hotel. A wedding Aria had organised, with Keynes's dedicated assistance, which made it the greatest celebration of all time because, you know, taste.

But it was all over now, and the prospect of long, uneventful months without a reason to force herself into Jen and Theo's happy life was... unappealing, to say the least. Not that she'd ever admit that. No-one needed to know how pathetic she'd become.

So instead, she offered a secondary truth. "Scouting for boys."

"Me too. But the pickings are slim."

"They are not," Aria snorted. She nodded toward a table of young men at the edge of the terrace, where the marble floor turned into La Christou's glorious patio. They were clearly appreciating the atmosphere, lounging around with casual grace, drinks in hand. Part of Theo's family; cousins, she thought. They shared his razor-sharp bone structure, and some of them were almost as handsome as he was. "They're gorgeous," she said. "Tell me they're not."

Keynes scoffed. "I've known those boys for too many years to take one to bed. I vaguely remember sharing a bath with the eldest."

Right; because Keynes and Theo's families were tight like that. Although it might be more accurate to say that Theo's family offered Keynes and his sister a respite from their nightmarish home life. Tomato, tomato.

"But," Keynes said, "any of them might do well for you, no?"

Once upon a time, she'd have thought the same. But that was before she'd learned the hard way just how dangerous her brand of 'romance' could easily become. "No-one here is doing it for me."

"Rubbish," he said. "You're just thinking about it too hard. You're not even drunk, are you?"

Stone cold sober—all the better to protect herself from her own desires. "Whatever," she replied, rolling her eyes. "You know, since I'm the maid of honour, I *should* be sleeping with the best man."

Keynes grinned, full lips parting to display American-white teeth. Honestly, the man had no right to look the way he did. If they were actors in a teen movie, he'd be the bad guy. He was too beautiful to be anything else. "Oh, love," he said. "If I were so inclined..."

"Blah, blah, blah. Stop trying to charm me. I'm not even

close to your type." Gender aside, Aria knew for a fact that Keynes preferred his partners... clean-cut.

Aria was as far from clean-cut as a country singer's mullet.

"Listen," he said. "You're moping, and we both know it. But look at all this." He swept a hand through the air, indicating the beauty around them—and the figures of Jenny and Theo, intertwined on the dance floor, swaying to every song as if it were a waltz. "Frankly, that slapped-arse expression is bringing down the mood. Want to take a break?"

The tip of Aria's tongue worried the silver ring bisecting her lower lip. "A break?"

"Yeah. Let's wander off. Go on an adventure. It'll be very Enid Blyton."

"Only Greek," she added, pushing off of the wall.

"Only Greek," he agreed, already leading the way.

"You know where you're going?"

"I know that you're following."

Well, she thought. *Fair enough.*

Nikolas Christou had a problem.

He wasn't really used to problems—which might be why he was handling this one so poorly. That was the downside to a charmed life, he reflected, as he jogged through his family's flagship hotel: a chronic inability to handle one's own shit.

Eventually, he'd have to learn. Maturity yawned out ahead of him, tapping its metaphorical foot, reminding him that his glory days were officially over. He'd have to grow up, now, wouldn't he?

But Christ, not tonight.

Nik had just retired—prematurely, to some, but not to his bank account—from pro football. The beautiful game had done something to his left knee that was, unfortunately, rather ugly. He'd come home to annoy his mother, harass his little sister, and decide what to do with the rest of his life, since he had no useful skills. He had not expected to bump into Melissa fucking Bright while licking his wounds.

Although, *bump into* seemed too generous a phrase. It was more accurate to say she'd hunted him down like a gazelle.

He could hear her voice now, echoing off the marble walls behind him. "Nik! Where are you? Did you see him, Perrie?" There was a pause, and then she practically shrieked, "NIK!"

His name on her lips had sounded so much better in bed. Strange, really.

He took a sharp right and hurried along the corridor. He certainly wasn't going to *run*—he did have some pride—but he couldn't be fucking bothered with this woman. Honestly, of all the questionable people he'd ever made the mistake of sleeping with, she was the absolute worst. Bloody exhausting, bless her. Though really, a part of him admired her tenacity.

But dealing with that tenacity usually gave him a migraine and made her, after she was done screaming, burst into tears. Nik hated to make a lady cry, even if that lady was a grasping, manipulative dingbat who couldn't take no for an answer. The thought of upsetting a woman made him imagine his tutting mother and scowling sister saying *God, Nik, you're so insensitive! Now look what you've done!*

He took a left, then a right, then another right, until he was tied up in knots. It was horrifying to realise how little he remembered of the hotel he'd grown up visiting; clearly, he'd been living and playing in England for too long. Melissa's voice chased him no matter which way he turned, growing closer and closer until she might as well be on top of him.

By the time he came across the deep, shadowed alcove bracketed by classical statuary, he was practically frantic. And by the time he noticed the two people *standing* in that alcove, staring at him as if he were a headless chicken, he was literally desperate.

He almost fell over in shock when he realised that one of the people was Keynes. Or rather, Olumide Olusegun-Keynes, man of the world, mystery, and excellent practical jokes.

Keynes's lips twitched as he took in Nik's panicked expression. "You alright, mate?"

"No," Nik said. He had never been one to prevaricate. "I am being ruthlessly corralled by a trio of lionesses."

Keynes gave in and allowed himself a full-blown smirk. At any other time, Nik might pause to admire the lips involved in that smirk.

The man as a whole was worthy of admiration, actually; he looked like a model, or maybe a wet dream. But that didn't matter, because Nik was—tragically—putting his days of carefree sluttery behind him.

"That's rough," Keynes said. Then he looked over at his companion, so of course, Nik did too. Which is when his jaw almost, very nearly, dropped.

Because the woman standing in the shadowed alcove was unlike anyone he'd ever seen.

He'd heard of people being called *striking*, and he certainly felt like he'd been struck. Her dress, long and buttercup-yellow, was pretty, but it was the rest of her that affected him most. Everything about her commanded attention, from the contrast between her platinum blonde hair and dark skin, to the tattoos that covered every visible inch of her. A silver ring glinted down the centre of her glossy lower lip, accompanied by little studs on either side of her nose and what looked like a thousand tiny gemstones decorating the curves of her ears.

She watched him with eyes rimmed in pitch-black makeup and glinting with amusement. There was a sardonic tilt to her lush mouth that made him think she was laughing *at* him, rather than with him. Then he heard Melissa's strident tones echoing from somewhere way-too-close, and the woman's slight smile turned into a full-blown, wicked grin. That grin was giving him ideas. But, worse than that, *something* about her was giving him fucking heart palpitations. He couldn't even describe the feeling that overtook him at the sight of her. It was like… like running onto a pitch and sprinting through icy drizzle, eyes narrowed, feet fast, the earth soft beneath his studs, knowing absolutely nothing could stop him.

Weird.

"In trouble?" she asked. And Jesus Christ, her low, teasing voice alone did more for Nik than porn ever had.

"You could say that," he managed, his eyes flitting from the smirk on her lips to the arch of her brow. She was tall, but the way she stood made her seem taller—or maybe it was the energy that surrounded her, strong enough to suffocate the weak.

Nik wasn't weak. But he wouldn't mind giving up his oxygen for her.

Which was possibly the strangest fucking thought he'd ever had.

"If you're a friend of Keynes's," she said, "then whatever's happening here must be your fault. He only likes disreputable people."

Nik heard, as if through a tunnel, the sound of Keynes snorting out a sarcastic response. He barely registered the words. He didn't register a damned thing except her, bright like sunshine, burning him alive in the most beautiful way. "If you're his friend, too," Nik said, "doesn't that make you disreputable?"

"Of course," she smiled. It was a real smile, so brilliant it set him off balance. Her brows arched as she grinned, one slightly higher than the other, and her eyes tilted up at the corners.

Nik didn't know if he'd just felt the earth shake or if he was actually losing his mind. Phantom or real, *something* jarred his bones and his brain all at once, until everything felt fundamentally... different.

He blinked slowly, readjusting to this slight shift in his world. Something inside him unfurled; it was the urgency that took over on the pitch, its demands a low growl. But for once, it wasn't telling him to win.

Her. Take her.

Wait, what?

Before he could grapple with that alarming thought, he heard the sharp click of footsteps. Melissa. His panicked caveman brain set in again. Actually, maybe it wasn't caveman brain, because a caveman's solution to this problem would be fight or flight, right?

As opposed to Nik's solution, which was to lock eyes with the tattooed woman and say, "Can I kiss you?"

Her brows shot up. "Me?"

"Yes."

"Now?"

"*Yes.*" When she didn't answer, he turned to Keynes. "Or you. If you're into that." He knew very well that Keynes *was* into that, but the woman beside him might not.

Keynes gave him a slow, catlike smile. "I certainly am." He stepped forward, hooked an arm around Nik's shoulders, and kissed him.

It was an excellent kiss, all things considered. But it didn't have the desired effect. Melissa didn't find Nik kissing someone else and finally take the fucking hint.

Instead, she saw him kissing someone else and hollered, "Nik! *There* you are!"

Aria had tried a lot of things, but she'd never bothered with voyeurism. It just didn't ring her bell.

She also knew that she wasn't the slightest bit attracted to Keynes. She had been, at one point, because he was drop-dead fucking gorgeous, but friendship had dealt with that lust rather swiftly.

Yet, as she watched Keynes kiss Mr. Tall, Tan and Terrified, she felt a hot, tight stirring in her belly that had been conspicuously absent for some time. And if it wasn't related to voyeurism, and it wasn't there because of Keynes, she supposed that only left one other source.

His friend. The stranger.

Which made sense, considering the way her eyes were currently devouring him. Her gaze danced feverishly from the swell of his biceps as he grabbed Keynes's arms, to the firm grip of those big, long-fingered hands, to the ferocious frown on his dark brow. A few seconds ago, his features had seemed sweet and friendly, despite his obvious panic. Now his profile was sharp, intense, hungry. She noticed abruptly that he was taller and more muscular than he'd seemed. She wouldn't have said, thirty seconds ago, that this guy was bigger than Keynes—but now she could see quite clearly that he was, because the two men were plastered together from mouth to hip.

You'd think that situation would put off the blonde woman who appeared a few feet away, with a pair of friends lagging just behind. But it didn't. Instead she stood for a moment, transfixed, her pink mouth forming a perfect O. Rather like a prim little version of Aria's own, she imagined.

But the woman's fixation didn't last quite as long as Aria's. She pulled herself together much more quickly, a smile taking over her face as she trilled, "Nik! *There* you are!"

At the sound of her voice, the stranger—Nik, apparently— stiffened. He broke the kiss, easing gently away from Keynes, a sort of grim resignation taking over his features. It was pretty obvious he'd hoped to make the woman disappear, for some reason, but she clearly wasn't that faint-hearted.

Typically, Aria was highly suspicious of men who ran from women. In her experience, that kind of situation suggested that a man had taken something, or else that he owed something, and in order to avoid dealing with his responsibilities, he was leading some poor cow on a merry chase.

But something about this particular man seemed so disturbingly... genuine. Or maybe she was just making excuses for herself. Maybe he was quite clearly scum, but her libido had taken over her brain. Whatever the reason, Aria did something deliciously reckless.

She stepped forward, caught the man's face in her hands, and brought her lips to his.

It wasn't difficult. Not just because she was tall and wearing killer heels besides—although that helped—but because he seemed totally onboard. Clearly, he was pretty fucking eager to avoid the woman standing a few feet away. Aria had just enough time to note that his eyelashes were ridiculously long, and his brown eyes looked almost black. Then his mouth was on hers and raw, needy lust rolled through her body like a tidal wave.

Kissing wasn't supposed to feel like this. Or rather, it was *supposed* to, but it never, ever did. In her nightly fantasies, a kiss would be enough to heat her blood, to sensitise her skin and send a shiver through her body, but in reality, it never was.

And yet, kissing the stranger did all that and more.

Maybe it was the way he held her; not settling his hands somewhere polite but wrapping both those thick arms around her waist and hauling her against him. Maybe it was the feel of his broad chest, his abdomen, his hips, pressed tight to hers. Maybe it was the fact that, despite the insistence of his touch, he kissed her almost gently. His lips moved over hers in a series of soft caresses. He didn't stick his tongue down her throat like an over-friendly dog. He didn't put his tongue in her mouth at all. Even though she kind of wanted him to.

That inappropriate desire reminded Aria that she was doing this for a reason. This guy wasn't kissing the hell out of her for kicks; he had an audience to perform for. To what end, she had no idea—but this kiss definitely made her Top 3 of All-Time list, so Aria decided she owed him.

He wanted to put on a show? She could do that. She could definitely, definitely do that.

Aria slid her hands from his jaw to the thick, silky strands of his hair, raking her fingers through it as she rolled her hips against his. She wasn't expecting him to release a soft groan against her lips, so quiet she almost missed it, but she certainly wasn't complaining. Not at all. She also couldn't complain when one of his hands began to roam, sliding down the small of her back, skipping her arse—*boo!*—but grabbing her thigh—*yay!*—and dragging her leg high.

At that point, her brain powered down completely to accommodate for all the extra blood her other body parts were demanding. And by 'other body parts' she meant her clit, which might as well be a bloody landmine. One touch and she'd explode. She'd better stop things here, because the arousal dancing along her nerve endings was starting to get out of hand.

Aria broke the kiss. Her vagina literally wept, but she did it anyway. Her vagina, after all, did not make the decisions here.

Her breath came in soft pants as she studied the face in front of her. The face of the man who'd just given her at least a month's worth of wanking material. He had golden skin, a broad nose and broader cheekbones, a square jaw and deep-set eyes that mirrored the shock she felt. Aria's gaze flicked down to his mouth without permission. His lips were full, slightly parted, bracketed by laugh lines. She wanted to taste them again.

"Gamóto," he breathed, the word harsh like a curse. "You— you're..."

Nice to know she wasn't the only one whose thoughts had been scattered by that lust tornado. But now probably wasn't the time for startled stuttering.

She tore her gaze away from him and turned to give the blonde woman a look. It wasn't her scariest look—not even close —but it *was* A Look. And it had the desired effect.

The woman didn't seem quite so unconcerned anymore. Her blue eyes were wide, her mouth tight, her hands curled into fists at her sides. She started to speak, a strangled, choked sound emerging from her lips. Then she snapped her mouth shut again. Finally, as Aria had expected, she turned on her heel and hissed, "Let's go!"

Her friends hurried off after her, tossing disgusted glares over their shoulders. As soon as they all disappeared, Aria took a step back, breaking free of the stranger's embrace—no matter how good his hands felt. He let her go, but the startled expression on his handsome face had turned into something more like awe.

"How did you *do* that?" he asked.

Aria shrugged. "Minor intimidation tactics. I'm a lot scarier than Keynes."

Keynes huffed out a laugh. "On sight, sure."

"But..." The stranger shook his head, frowning down at her long, yellow skirts. "You're not scary at all. You look like a princess."

Aria's brows flew up. Beside her, Keynes gaped at the man standing in front of them, his jaw as slack as hers felt. This guy must be taking the piss, right? But he looked genuinely confused, and completely earnest, and...

And it didn't matter if he needed his eyes testing; she had a conscience to soothe and places to be. "Listen, before I rush back to the ballroom—" that quip was rewarded by Keynes's snicker "—I kind of want to know what just happened. You aren't, like, avoiding child maintenance payments, are you?" The stranger wrinkled his nose. "What? No. I'm avoiding Melissa. She's not great at taking no for an answer. But this tactic went *much* more smoothly."

Aria digested that nonsensical speech, decided it was bull-shit, then turned to look at Keynes. To her surprise, he didn't offer a mocking smirk, or roll his eyes. Instead, he nodded subtly, as if to say, *"The bullshit you just heard is totally legit, by the way."*

Aria puzzled over this for a second before deciding that Keynes, despite being her friend, was a man, and therefore not entirely trustworthy.

Ah, well. She didn't need to know the truth, anyway. "We should get back to the reception."

"We certainly should," Keynes agreed. He slung an arm over her shoulder, and they walked away.

"Wait!" the stranger called. "Hang on a second." He had a slight accent, and it seemed to grow more pronounced as he followed them. "What's your name?"

"Aria," she said, still walking. It wasn't exactly classified information.

"I'm Nik. Nikolas. Aria, I want to—"

"I'm busy," she called over her shoulder. "Hence the whole *walking away* thing."

"Tomorrow, then!"

She laughed as Keynes propelled her down the hall. "If you can find me!"

The sound of his heavy footsteps behind them ceased. Just before she turned the corner towards the ballroom, he spoke again. "I will. I'll find you."

Beside her, Keynes gave a quiet snort. "Oh, Nik. That boy. He sounds like a bloody Disney hero."

Aria laughed softly, and they shared a congenial smirk at the stranger's expense. Only, she couldn't help but remember that, five minutes ago, he'd called her a princess.

So, it made sense that he sounded like a prince.

Chapter 2

Retiring from Slutdom

N ik spent the night kicking irritably at his sheets, scowling at his ceiling in the dark, and replaying that damned kiss. The possessive beast in his chest didn't let up for a second, demanding that he go and fetch her. Fetch Aria. *Aria.* He recalled the sweet pressure of her mouth on his, those full lips and the bite of that piercing; the lush feel of her body, the way his fingers had sunk into her thigh...

He'd never wanted anyone like this. He'd never wanted any*thing* like this, not even his career, because frankly, he'd never been hungry. Nik was painfully aware of the fact that he'd sailed through life without effort, from spoilt brat to gifted teen to successful adult, all based on his family background and his natural athleticism. He'd never lain awake at night wondering if he'd gain whatever his heart desired, because he always knew that he would.

Nik Christou saw, wanted, and took. But he couldn't just *take* a woman. And the knowledge was frustrating him like nothing else. Maybe that was why he spent the last few drowsy hours before dawn fantasising about her taking him.

Whatever was causing this strange obsession, it didn't

matter. The salient point, Nik decided, was that he needed Aria. Ever since he'd ended his contract with Colston City, Nik had been treading a tightrope over shark-infested waters. The sharks were anxiety, the waters depression; when he fell, he'd be eaten alive if he didn't drown first. And every day that passed without his teammates, without his profession, without the only thing that had ever made him useful, Nik's balance slipped a little more.

But around her, he'd been on solid ground. That, he'd realised, was the feeling that had shaken him. The sensation of earth beneath his feet at last.

Yeah. He needed her. Badly.

Nik was up bright and early the next morning, prowling the halls for a flash of platinum hair and silver piercings. Unfamiliar nerves stalked him, a sense of low-level dread caused by the instinctive knowledge that if he found her and fucked up somehow, he would regret it.

The solution was simple, then: he would not fuck this up.

Since that was settled, Nik continued his search, greeting the staff as he went. Most of them didn't answer his nods and cheerful *Kaliméras* because they were too busy gaping at the sight of Nik Christou out and about before sunset. He'd been almost nocturnal since his fucking knee had stolen his only passion from him. He may have indulged in a depression nap or five, as his sister called them.

But he'd recently—just last night, in fact—rediscovered his winning mentality and decided that it was time to start a new phase in his life. A different career, another direction. Maybe something philanthropic. He promised himself that by the time he figured things out completely, he'd have Aria's number at the very least. It might be a challenge, but that was okay.

Nik was always, *always,* up for a challenge.

He found the source of his small-scale meltdown in the

hotel's breakfast buffet, her platinum hair smoothed back into a little ponytail, her attention focused on the piles food in front of her. When Nik saw her, he stopped in his tracks. Looking at this woman felt like stepping out of an air-conditioned building into the heat of summer; like being smacked by a wall of heat. But this heat had little to do with the temperature, and everything to do with the sight of her bare legs beneath the table. Nik sent up a quick prayer of thanks for the invention of short shorts. Then he stared some more.

She looked up, obviously feeling his gaze, and scowled.

Which was not the reaction Nik typically received from people he'd kissed. It certainly wasn't the reaction he wanted from the woman he appeared to be obsessed with, but life was not for the faint-hearted. He made his way over to her table and sat down.

She gave him a flat stare while chewing on a croissant. He briefly fantasised about licking off the smudge of scarlet jam hovering at the edge of her lip, then decided that would be coming on too strong.

"Found you," he said.

She swallowed her mouthful. "Whoopee."

Ouch. But he was pleasantly distracted from that sting when her tongue snaked out to lick away the smudge of jam he'd been eyeing. Watching her do it was *almost* as good as doing it himself. He imagined.

But enough of his imaginings. He wasn't good at talking to people, not romantically. He had no practice, since he typically didn't have to try. This conversation, therefore, would require all of his concentration. "Good morning," he said, offering his most charming smile. All of his smiles were charming, according to his agent, but this one was definitely the best.

She nodded, a sort of jerky head-tilt that only went up, rather than down. "Hi."

He was surprised she'd responded at all, considering the extra-strength aura of *fuck off* she was giving out. Truthfully, after last night's kiss, that aura might as well have been a dog whistle. When it came to her, he was definitely a fucking dog.

"I'm sorry to intrude on your breakfast," he began, "but I wanted to thank you for what you did yesterday. It was kind of you to help me when we are strangers."

Aria sighed as if considering a great tragedy. "I don't know what I was thinking, to be honest."

"I believe you must be softer at heart than you'd like."

She glared at him. Nik shifted subtly in his chair and decided that later, he'd take a moment to examine why her glares made him hard. Right now, though, he'd just have to go with it. "You're a very impressive woman. I'd like to get to know you better."

She rolled her eyes and picked up a bunch of grapes. "I've heard that before."

His lips twitched. "I bet." The array of dishes before her was so massive, it covered his side of the table as well as hers. It was as if she'd made her own little buffet within the buffet. Since he was always starving, courtesy of his unholy metabolism, Nik reached for a slice of cheese as he spoke. "Really, though. I think—"

"Wooooah," she said, reaching out to slap his hand. "Don't touch my food, man."

He gaped. "Are you serious? You have an absolute mountain on this table. You're never going to eat this."

"It's *my* mountain. And you don't know what I can eat. If I see your hand on this food again, I'll stab it." She raised her fork, apparently serious. "I know where all the important tendons are."

He must be fucked up, because the sight of Aria waving a fork with violent intent was making him want to smile. He

22

really had no idea why people apparently found her intimidating. She was adorable. And lickable. And funny. And so, so lickable. He dropped the cheese.

"Good boy," she said, slicing into her eggs. "Now, since you're taking all fucking day to spit this out, let me speed things up."

Oh, wonderful. She was going to cut right through his strange brand of social awkwardness. They really were made for each other.

"You're after a repeat of last night's avoidance routine," Aria said. "Right?"

He blinked. "I beg your pardon?"

She gave him an arch look. "Keynes told me all about you. Apparently, you really are drowning in genitalia of all sorts. He reckons you're too nice to say no to people."

Well, that was arguably true. But... "That's why you think I'm here?"

She raised her brows, looking genuinely confused. "Is that... *not* why you're here?"

"I just..." He paused, considering. He couldn't run his mouth as usual, not in this situation, not with her. He needed to tread carefully, to find out what she thought. "It wouldn't be unreasonable for you to assume that I came to find you with a different goal in mind, would it? A more personal goal."

A look of horror crossed her face. "You're not asking me out, are you?" she demanded.

"No," he said quickly. Because he certainly fucking wasn't, not if the prospect made her look like *that*.

"Oh." She rolled her eyes, almost at herself, and smiled slightly. "Sorry. Keynes did tell me that you don't date."

Keynes talked too fucking much. "That's true. I don't." *But if you'd like to change that, feel free.*

"Cool." She took a moment to chew on a few bites of egg,

her expression thoughtful. Meanwhile, Nik sat in silence and tried to figure out how to keep her with him at all times, forever-and-ever-amen, if she wouldn't even let him take her out. He may have to get creative. That was okay. He worked best under pressure.

Finally, she swallowed, took a huge gulp of orange juice, and focused on him again. "So, you want, like, an escort?"

Ah, yes. His quest for a human shield, which she had somehow invented entirely on her own. "*Are* you an escort?" How much did escorts charge? Could he conceivably hire her for... the rest of his life?

"Never done it before," she said cheerfully, "but everyone starts somewhere, right? No, I'm actually a tattoo artist." She raised one heavily inked arm, waving it about like a prop rather than a limb. "And, you know, a walking cliché."

"There is nothing cliché about you," he murmured. As soon as the words left his mouth, he realised he'd said them all wrong. They were too fervent, too earnest, too fucking obvious. But her self-deprecation made him want to outline her perfection in detail. With his tongue. Between her legs.

Just an idea.

Clearing his throat, Nik moved on. "So, you're not an escort, but you *are* open to fulfilling this... this need I have?" Christ, that sounded terrible. But it also sounded like an excellent fucking idea. He could hire her to stay by his side, they'd get to know each other, some stuff would occur—he was hazy on that part of the plan, but he assumed it would involve charming the pants off of her—and *boom*. She'd be in his life, eventually in his bed, and hopefully at least half as into him as he was into her. He might even accept a quarter. An eighth, perhaps. Because he was pretty fucking into her.

With a smirk, she asked, "Do you need someone to protect

you from the horror of pretty girls who want you bad? Oh, and boys?"

"It's usually the women," he admitted. The words weren't a lie, but Nik was uncomfortably aware that the conversation had taken a... misleading turn. He didn't need anyone to protect him from sex.

Although, actually, he kind of did. Because he *was* leaving his days of carefree sluttery behind him, and he *did* have trouble telling people to fuck off, and he also had the strangest feeling that if he tried to sleep with anyone but Aria, it might not work. Where was this feeling coming from? Nik had no idea. But his father had always said, *"Trust your gut"*.

Also, *"Don't kick that damned football in my damned house."* But that mantra didn't really apply here, and Nik had never listened to it anyway.

So, he pushed down his disquiet and decided to go with Aria's insinuations, to let the conversation take the path she seemed to expect. "When people are especially determined, they struggle to accept refusals. Which usually means I have to be unkind. I hate to be unkind, but especially to women. Hence last night's fiasco."

She cocked her head. "Especially to women?"

"Well, men are brutes. But all my life, women have been so sweet to me. And they are delicate."

Aria gave a derisive snort, flicking a few stray platinum hairs out of her eyes. There were ink stains all over her fingers. "You do realise that's incredibly reductionist, right?"

He had no idea what that meant. She was, apparently, smarter than him. He was not surprised. "It's what?"

She rolled her eyes, speaking slowly for his benefit. "Do I look delicate to you?"

Nik studied the little curve of flesh that spilled out between her arm and the strap of her vest. Then he eyed the dip in the bridge of her nose, the tilt at the edge of her lips, the way she angled her head just an inch to the right. "Yes."

Aria coughed. Coughed some more. Grabbed a glass of water and choked it down. "Oh. Right. Okay."

"To be frank, I cannot make a woman cry."

"I highly doubt that any woman would cry because you refused to have sex with her." He didn't say anything, but something must have shown in his face, because a second later she spluttered, "Oh my God. Seriously? Are you serious? Women cry because you won't have sex with them?"

"Not all the time."

"What the hell have you got down there, fucking Excalibur?"

"I don't believe size matters," he said.

Aria stared. "I don't believe you're serious."

"About size?"

"About anything."

Well. In all fairness, that wasn't generally inaccurate.

"However, this is an interesting problem you claim to have." She brought a little bunch of grapes to her lips. He watched, every muscle in his body tensing, as she sucked a grape from its stem with a *pop*. Fuck. "Sounds more like you need a 24/7 bodyguard."

What he needed was a position Aria could fill that kept her by his side at all times, or at least long enough for him to have a chance with her. For a moment, reality seemed suspended, as if he'd found himself at a crossroads.

Are you really about to do this? Because it doesn't seem wise.

I want her.

She doesn't want you. Let her turn you away. Better than lying, isn't it?

He didn't know. He wasn't sure.

Give up, the voice whispered.

He didn't know where that voice was coming from, but it had just said the wrong fucking thing. Nikolas Christou did not give up. Ever. He certainly wasn't going to start by giving up on her.

Time restarted, life and sound blooming around him. Aria watched him expectantly, that ever-playful gleam in her dark eyes. He still didn't know if she was laughing with him or at him. Did it matter, when the sight of her satisfaction felt like a reward in itself?

"In six weeks, my friend Alvaro is hosting a seven-day house party in Marbella," he said. "It's an annual thing, with my team." His *old* team. He'd attend Varo's blowout party one last time. And then he'd be done. Ready to face the next stage of his life, whatever it may be. "I want to go, but I can't be bothered with everyone I've ever slept with expecting a repeat performance. So..." The words flowed easily, as if a devil were speaking through him. "So, I need you to pose as my girlfriend. To help, the way you did last night."

Did it count as a lie if he kind of meant it, the moment he said it? No. Obviously not.

This isn't why you came here. You're misleading her.

Shut up.

Aria narrowed her eyes suspiciously. "And you don't want to sleep with anyone because..."

Because I know you, and now the thought of touching someone else is making me feel slightly sick. "It's complicated. I just retired—"

"From slutdom?"

Nik choked back a laugh. "From football." He paused to see if that interested her at all. Nope; she was still focused on her pastry. Strange, for an Englishwoman. "I've decided to take this opportunity to overhaul my life. I'm turning over a new leaf,

27

choosing a more mature path, not shagging everything with a pulse, etcetera. Which is where you come in."

She stared, and he had the oddest feeling that she could see directly into his head. Nerves skated along his spine, a sensation he'd only ever felt before a match. This odd attachment he'd formed was fucking stressful, and it'd barely been twenty-four hours. Maybe if he just ignored it, if he left her alone and tried to forget they'd ever met, these tumultuous, indescribable feelings would pass.

But something inside him snarled violently at the idea. Hm. That was out of the question, then.

Finally, she opened her mouth to speak. Which, of course, was when the waiter came.

Aria had breakfast to eat, a flight to catch, and exactly 0.00 grams of patience to spare for *I get too much sex* sob stories. It was a shame that such a disarmingly sexy man—a man so sexy she'd spent all night thinking about a goddamn kiss like a bloody teenager—was so utterly full of shit. But also, entirely expected.

She was just about to tell Nik he could go fuck himself when a waiter appeared, holding an enormous silver tray. The waiter nodded politely at Aria and murmured, "Madam," before giving Nik a huge smile. Then he started unloading even more food onto the little table, taking Aria's empty plates as he went.

"Efcharistó, fíle," Nik said, grinning back at the waiter like they were old friends. He dug into a bowl of cornflakes while the guy backed away.

"Did you order that?" she asked, while sitting in a hotel breakfast buffet where no-one could order anything.

"No." Nik bit into a slice of toast.

"Do you... come here a lot?"

He looked up at her, as if in surprise. "My mother owns the hotel." He pointed to himself. "Nik Christou. Did I mention that? I thought I mentioned that."

She stared.

He ate some fried tomatoes.

"You... are... a hotel owner," she said finally.

"No. I'm a footballer. I'm a *retired* footballer."

"Well, Jesus, pick a wealth source. That's just greedy."

He blinked. "The hotel isn't mine. I don't—"

"Oh, for God's sake, never mind. Look, I don't know what you want from me—"

"But I told you. I want you to be my scary fake girlfriend during a week-long party at Alvaro's house in Marbella." He grimaced. "I'm not good with social situations, to be honest. If it weren't for my position and my..." He waved a hand in the air, probably to indicate his excellent body, beautiful face, and general sex appeal. "Truthfully, I'd never get anyone into bed. I don't know how to speak to people. All I do is kick balls around and make bad decisions. I certainly have no idea how to let people down gently."

He managed to say all this in a manner that sounded slightly self-deprecating, mostly amused, and somehow appealing. Or maybe that last part was more related to his smile, with those full lips and that strong, square jaw, and the way his eyes crinkled up at the corners. Whatever.

"If I'm honest," he said, leaning forward in a way that made his broad shoulders seem like a brick fucking wall, "I have lived a charmed life. It has made me quite thoughtless, I think. I would sit back, and sex would fall into my lap. So, I took it. But really, that's no way for a grown man to behave, now, is it?"

As if hypnotised, Aria found herself shaking her head slowly. "No," she murmured, while her brain shouted, *Why are you agreeing with him like any of this makes sense? He is every-*

thing you should be wary of in this world, and he is feeding you the biggest crock of shit you've ever been fed!

Well. Except for the crock of shit Simon had fed her. Because nothing, Aria thought, could ever be so terrible as finding out that her boyfriend was actually a murderous stalker. So maybe she shouldn't be too hard on Nik right now.

"So, you agree!" he said. "You understand!"

Of course she didn't bloody understand. How could anyone possibly be so bad at saying *No* that they needed a fake fucking girlfriend to protect them from sex?

But then she remembered the panicked look on his face when she'd first seen him last night. And the way that soft, smiling mouth had turned grim when he'd thought he'd have to speak to whatsherface—Melissa. And, come to think of it, the way Melissa had chased him down, despite the fact that he was quite literally running away.

Maybe there were some downsides to being rich and gorgeous. And, Aria realised, potentially famous. She had no idea. She wasn't into football.

"I kind of see where you're coming from," she admitted. "But 'understand' might be a strong word."

He smiled. "Fair enough." For a moment his expression turned oddly serious. It transformed his face from sweet and gentle to painfully intense. She didn't like intensity. Except, apparently, on him. "It's just that this party is important. I want to see my teammates again and pretend my life hasn't turned on its head. That's all. I don't need the complications."

Now, *that* she could understand. Aria was astonished to realise that she was starting to take him seriously, starting to actually consider this proposal. Which was absurd. And ill-advised. She shook her head irritably. "Look, I'm sorry, but I'm not running off to Marbella with some random footballer."

"I'm not random," he said hotly. "I've never missed the World Cup squad."

She pursed her lips to hide a smile. "That's great. Well done, sugar. I still have no fucking clue who you are, and 'double-wealthy playboy beloved by all' is not the greatest character reference."

Surprisingly, he seemed enthused by that rather than offended. "Get to know me, then. We have six weeks. Spend them with me."

Spend six weeks with a guy who'd gotten her wet with a single fucking kiss? And then spend another week as his fake girlfriend at some millionaire party in Spain? Aria had a history of making poor decisions—very poor decisions—but she wasn't completely lacking in brain cells. "No."

His face fell. "No?"

He looked so adorably disappointed, it almost hurt her heart. In fact, it *did*, like a tiny little arrow digging into vital flesh. Which was odd, since she didn't actually think she had a heart. Just a gaping hole in her chest that was always ravenous and eternally empty, no matter how hard she tried to fill it.

See, this was why she embraced the whole *princess of darkness* thing. Sometimes, her brain came out with shit so depressing, it was almost poetic.

Still, the look on Nik's face was unsettling enough that she found herself trying to fix it. "Maybe we could... email?" she offered. That was safe, right? Because, sure, when she looked at him, her pulse hummed with a rhythm that sounded a lot like *Mine*—but if he wasn't actually *there*, that pesky beat would stop.

"Email," he agreed. "Yes. Yes. Let's do that. You're smart."

Aria had been fawned over by many men, but never one quite so handsome as him. Definitely not one who radiated raw sexuality like it was fucking cologne. The experience almost distracted her from the question she'd finally thought to ask.

"I'm assuming this... *position* would be paid." She knew it would be paid. It *better* be paid. Because he was clearly loaded and slightly soft, and she had bills to deal with. So, so many bills.

"Of course," he said. "I've never really done this before, but I was thinking £100,000."

She shoved a forkful of eggs into her mouth to hide the fact that her jaw had dropped. Then she thought about the fact that, since Jen had moved out of their shared flat—and since a murderous stalker had covered their walls with blood—Aria was now living with her parents. Her Bible-bashing parents who quoted Leviticus every time she got a new tattoo, along with her teenage sisters, who were, at best, shrill. Then she thought about the tattoo apprenticeship she'd completed, and, for that matter, how much she wanted to open her own studio.

Also, she thought about the latest lip gloss collection from Dior.

She said, "£350,000."

"Okay," he replied. Just like that.

Fuck. *Fuck.* He was a footballer, for Christ's sake. He probably made millions. She should've asked for more.

Wait—what the hell was she doing? Aria shook her head sharply, the reality of her situation falling like a ton of bricks. "You can't be serious. This is not serious. This—"

"Google me," he sighed. "I have the money. I play for Colston City. Google me."

"I don't want to fucking Google you," she hissed across the table. "I don't care if you have all the money in the fucking world! In fact, that just makes this even worse! Worse, and incredibly weird, and frankly dangerous!"

He stared at her as if she'd just climbed on top of the table and laid an egg. "Dangerous?"

"Yes! Because you are a man, and you're wealthy and powerful. You giving me a lot of money for an incredibly odd arrangement would create a questionable situation between us. You could probably defend yourself in court by saying we agreed upon all kinds of shit, and that's why you paid so much—"

"Wait, wait," he interjected, brows shooting up. "*Court?* What do you think I'm going to do?"

"I don't know *what* you're going to do," she shot back. "That's the point! I don't know you, I don't trust you, and I wouldn't have any guarantees in an arrangement like that!"

"First of all," he said calmly, "you're friends with Keynes, right? Well, so am I. He knows I'm not a secret murderer, or anything. And secondly, you would have guarantees. You'd have a contract."

Aria sat back as her adrenaline drained away, leaving something shaky and anti-climactic in its wake. "A... contract?"

"Of course. I'm not just going to give you all that money out of nowhere. My accountant would throttle me, for one thing. This is a job. I'm totally prepared to do this aboveboard." He paused. "Although there would be an NDA, I suppose. You have a lawyer, right?"

She almost laughed at that. "I don't know if you can tell, but I'm a normal person. You know, poor. Poor people don't have lawyers."

He appeared to be holding back a smile. "I know. I was talking about Keynes."

Oh, yes. Their mutual friend Keynes, who was, incidentally, a solicitor. "Whatever," she muttered. "Fine. Yes, I have a lawyer."

"Good," he said.

"But I'm telling you now." Aria waved her fork threateningly. "Don't fuck with me. You'll regret it. My uncle is a big-time gangster, you know, back home." Her uncle was a used car salesman with an overbite from Lowdham.

Either way, Nik didn't appear scared. Instead he seemed... concerned. His dark eyes turned gentle, almost as if he knew why she felt the need to say all this. As if he knew something had happened to her, that she'd once been a fearless woman and now she was only ever afraid.

"I'm asking you to help me," he said softly. "I wouldn't hurt *anyone*, but I'd never hurt someone who was trying to help me. And I'd rather die than hurt you."

He looked so sweet, with those huge brown eyes, that soft, smiling mouth, and those big hands clutching a tiny mug of tea. She almost believed him.

But Aria, she reminded herself, was a terrible judge of character.

Dear Aria,

You mentioned (correctly) that we should get to know each other before we do this thing. And I thought, what better way to show you my deepest, truest self than a compilation of my favourite Vines? Please find attached.

Yours,

Nik

Dear Nik,

You are, of course, right about me being right. And I agree that Vines are an important insight to the soul.

Which is why I'm sadly disappointed to find key, iconic Vines missing from your compilation. Either your research was shoddy, or your soul is underdeveloped. Please find attached a reflection of my own soul, and a far superior offering.

Best,

Aria

Dear Aria,

I want to argue, but your compilation is, in fact, way better than mine. See, I'm all about sportsmanship. I can lose gracefully. However, I will not take this loss lying down. You may regret the day you ever dared to best me in anything remotely resembling a competition. Because you and I will now be trapped in this contest forever, while I do everything I can to prove myself the ultimate Vine master.

To that end, please find attached another compilation. If you can give better than that, hit me.

Nik

Dear Nik,

It's on.

Chapter 3

A Shit in a Showroom Toilet

Six Weeks Later

> Remember to text me the address!!!

> Don't worry, I will. We just arrived, so I'll send it soon. x

Jennifer wasn't usually a triple-exclamation-mark kind of gal, but she was clearly feeling anxious about her best friend travelling to Spain with a retired footballer to pose as his fake girlfriend. Well, actually, Jen didn't know about that, because Aria had signed an NDA. So, she was *really* anxious about Aria, known lover of fuck boys and literally murderous men, flitting off on a 'romantic holiday' with a 'new boyfriend' no-one but Keynes had ever met.

Which meant that Aria had to text Jen constantly this week, just to confirm her continued survival and ease her poor friend's worry.

It was a damned good thing she was getting paid for this, or she'd be annoyed already.

Of course, the sultry heat of a Spanish afternoon went some way to alleviating that annoyance. So did the massive 4x4 whose passenger seat she currently occupied, and the huge gated villa the car was pulling up to... and even the man in the driver's seat.

Not that she liked Nikolas Christou, or anything—even if he was kind of funny over email. She didn't like him at all. Theirs was a strictly professional relationship. But God, on a physical level, Aria liked him a hell of a fucking lot.

From behind the cover of her Victoria Beckham-esque shades (circa 2006, since Nik was a footballer and all), Aria devoured the man sitting beside her. His attention was on the cool, shadowy garage they were rolling into. His head was tilted back slightly, and his full lips were parted in a way that reminded her of, say, a guy looking down at her as she sucked his cock. Just for example.

He had one big hand wrapped around the gearstick, the other on the wheel. His forearms were golden-brown and dusted with dark hair, thickly muscled and lined with veins she'd love to run her tongue over. Theoretically, of course. Just like she was *theoretically* wondering which of the many toys in her sox—aka her sex box—might be the exact same size as his long, thick fingers. All in the name of science, you understand.

But Aria did not like Nik at all.

He parked the car and looked at her. It wasn't the way normal people looked, with eyes and general attention and all that. It was some next-level, ridiculously intense look that she'd only ever seen from Nik. He met her gaze and she felt like she'd been slapped in the face with *feelings*. Like he was telepathically pushing shit into her brain, shit like, *You're special,* and *You're the centre of my world,* and *Holy fuck, I care so much about everything that comes out of your mouth.*

He put all that in her head with a sweep of those thick lashes, and then he followed it up with the utterly mundane: "You good?"

Nik, Aria had quickly realised, was one of *those* men. You

know; the ones who'd been born with the superpower of effortless seduction, who could make you believe they'd fallen in love by fucking accident. She'd decided to keep that fact at the forefront of her mind all week, like armour in the battle against those big brown eyes. "I'm good," she nodded.

He smiled at her as they got out of the car, and Aria's so-called armour collapsed. Oh, dear Lord, why did he have to be so fine? Why? What was the reason? Who made him? Where did he come from? It simply wasn't natural.

"Everyone will be asleep," he said while she had a mental crisis over his hotness. "Except G, maybe. She gets up early."

Aria cast a doubtful look at the bright Spanish sun beyond the opening of the garage. "Asleep?"

"Party started yesterday, technically."

She hadn't expected Nik to grab her luggage at the airport—rich men were generally thoughtless—but he had. So, she wasn't surprised when he did the same thing now, hauling both their suitcases out of the car as if it were nothing. His might actually be pretty light, but Aria knew full well that hers was weighed down by vital outfit changes, shoe options, assorted belly bars, and a hell of a lot of sex toys. Like she'd ever leave the sox at home when she was fake-dating the guy who'd melted her knickers off with a kiss. What did she look like, a fool?

He led the way into the house, its air conditioning delicious against her slightly sweaty skin. Was Spain supposed to be this fucking hot? It wasn't *that* far from home. She stretched out her arms as they wandered through cool, dim hallways. "Who's G, by the way?"

Before Nik could answer, a sickly-sweet voice came from a nearby room. "I'm G! Who's you?" A second later, a figure appeared in the doorway.

A very short, very *thin* figure in a tiny red bikini that matched her scarlet lipstick and complimented her waist-length, golden hair. The woman widened incredible baby blues at the sight of them. Then, without waiting for a response to her question, she gave an excitable squeal and ran up to Nik with open arms.

Which was when Aria's travel-fatigued brain made use of the info Nik had been feeding her for weeks. 'G' must be *Georgia*, Nik's best friend's girl, a woman firmly on the 'safe' list. Which meant Aria didn't have to beat her off with a stick.

Good thing, too. It'd be pretty damn hard to get a stick, or a ruler, or a blade of fucking grass, between Nik and Georgia's bodies right now.

Not that Aria was jealous. Her concern was purely professional. She was, after all, a professional girlfriend.

As if he'd heard that thought, Nik stepped back and turned to Aria. He held out a hand, flashing a smile that would have turned her brain to mush *if* she weren't in possession of certain important facts. Like the fact that everything about to occur between them would be 100% staged.

Still, his hand sliding into hers felt real enough. In fact, it shocked her system like a bolt of lightning.

"Ri," he said, and she realised he was talking to *her*. Ri? Fucking *Ri*? Aria would have been disgusted by such rampant shortening of her name, if it didn't vaguely connect her to the legend that was Rihanna. "This is Georgia," Nik went on. "Georgia, this is my girlfriend, Aria."

For a second, Georgia's mouth hung open. It was a rather impactful sight, what with all the red lipstick involved. But a heartbeat later she pulled herself together and gave Aria a smile that seemed totally genuine.

"Oh my God!" she trilled. "*Girlfriend?*" But not in a bitchy kind of way. More like the way someone would shout, "*Oh my God, is that a fresh pack of Digestives?*" Then she threw herself into Aria's arms just as she'd thrown herself at Nik. It was quite a strange sensation, having a tiny, half-naked stranger hanging on to her waist, but Aria decided it wasn't completely unpleasant.

"Hi," she managed.

Georgia stepped back. "You alright, babe? Oh, I'm proper buzzing to meet you!" She turned an exasperated look on Nik and said, "Did you tell Varo about this? Cuz if you've told him, and he ain't told me—"

"Calm down," Nik said. "I didn't mention it. Didn't want to cause a fuss. Aria's very private." This was the line they had agreed upon.

"Oohhhhh," Georgia said. She gave Aria a sympathetic look. "I *completely* understand. I was just saying to Laurie yesterday —you'll meet Laurie, when she drags her arse out of bed." Georgia launched into a truly astonishing cackle that lasted approximately three seconds before ending abruptly. "I was saying, people overshare so much these days. Especially with social media. No-one needs to know if me and Varo are nipping down the beach for a shag, do you know what I mean? That's not IG story material! But some people, oh, I could go on all day."

"Really," Nik agreed solemnly. "She could."

Georgia tossed her acres of sunshine hair in a disdainful sort of way and said, "Shush, you!" Then she turned back to Aria. "So, what's going *on*? How did this *happen*? Where did youse *meet*?" She grinned like a kid awaiting a bedtime story.

Aria offered her best impression of shyness—which wasn't great, since she'd never been shy—and said, "Oh, it's kind of a funny story."

A story she'd rehearsed several times, in preparation for this moment. They'd decided to stick close to the truth, but Nik kept harping on about *delivery*. Apparently, they had to be convincing, or his friends wouldn't believe a word of it. He'd never had a girlfriend before, or a boyfriend, for that matter, so he predicted shock.

Clearly, when it came to relationships, the two of them were polar opposites.

But Aria intended to earn her hundreds of thousands of pounds—damn, those words felt good, even in her mind—so she was ready to put on the best performance of her life. Until Nik pulled her into his arms so suddenly she forgot how to breathe.

"She kissed me," he said, staring down at her with more love in his eyes than she'd seen from her own damn mother. "We bumped into each other at the hotel, and she just... grabbed me and kissed me."

It was disturbingly easy to melt against his broad chest, to smile up at him in fond, mock-censure. "You *asked* me to kiss you, Nik."

"And I thought you were going to say no."

"I didn't say anything. I was thinking."

"Well, you took your bloody time," he said, sounding for all the world like a sheepish, smitten bastard.

"But I got there in the end," Aria replied, her voice sickeningly soft. She hadn't known she could act like this. She was almost scaring herself. If the look on her face was even close to the adoring stare on his, they both deserved an Oscar. A joint Oscar. Was that a thing? Well, it should be.

"Oh my God!" Georgia squealed, clapping her hands together. She jumped up and down, and her magnificent chest bounced like a pair of melons rolling down someone's front steps. Aria mentally filed the image away for the boob job she was never going to get, but constantly considered. "*You*," Georgia cried, pointing at Nik, "are in love!"

Nik's reaction wasn't half as negative as it should be. "Oh, come on, G," he said cheerfully. "Don't stress me." But Aria caught his cocky little wink. And she definitely caught the way he looked down at her through those thick, sooty lashes, dragging his teeth over that lush lower lip.

As if he were ready to fall.

"I think that went well," Nik said, as he set down their suitcases and shut the bedroom door firmly. They were in the room Varo usually gave him, right at the top of the house and *almost* alone, but complete privacy was necessary. No point hiring a (fake) fake girlfriend if anyone could pass by and overhear the fact that she was, you know, fake.

When Aria didn't answer, he turned to find her standing in the middle of the room, staring at the queen-sized bed. Nik smiled and ran a hand through his hair, stretching out the aching muscles in his back. "Yeah, the room's amazing. I love this house."

Abruptly, Aria turned to him, her focus on the bed forgotten. "What was that?"

Nik's smile faded. He wasn't exactly an expert in social interaction, but her tone did not sound positive. "What was what?"

"That. Down there. I know the point is to fake this, but..." she gave a brittle, nervous sort of laugh. "I didn't know you were that good an actor."

"Was I... supposed to be bad?" Nik asked slowly. Then he realised what he was saying and frowned. "Wait, what? I don't get it. What's the problem?"

For a moment, she just looked at him with something steely in her gaze. She was beautiful, of course, even after the flight. He was starting to think she couldn't *not* be beautiful. Her hair was dark now and longer than it had been when they met. She was wearing shorts and a vest, but the *way* she wore them—he couldn't even describe it. Something about her commanded attention, and it was sexy as hell.

At that moment, though, she seemed fragile despite her power. She wrapped her arms around herself and watched him almost warily, as if expecting him to turn into a monster before her eyes. The tension swelled for several rigid seconds. But then she shook her head and slowly seemed to relax.

"Sorry," she said. "I don't know what I'm going on about. You just shocked me. I didn't know you could lie like that."

He grimaced at the word. *Lie.* He hadn't felt as if he was lying downstairs, but he supposed he must've been. And he was definitely lying to her, kind of. Sort of. Was paying an extortionate amount of money to keep her with him under false pretences a lie?

No. That is the behaviour of a potential serial killer.

Oh, for God's sake.

"It was easy," he admitted, "to... perform love. Because I've seen so much of it. My parents, before my father died. My sister and her husband. I wouldn't say I'm a good liar, but that I can do."

The last bit of hesitancy left her expression. "That's sweet. I wish I could say the same," she chuckled, wandering around the room, from the ornate vanity he'd never used to the huge, glass-panelled wardrobe. "My parents fucking hate each other."

The humour in her voice startled a laugh out of him. He almost forgot the unease that had cloaked her moments earlier; in fact, *she* seemed to have forgotten it. Maybe it was just nerves. It was easy to forget that she could feel something so mundane, because everything about Aria was bold and fearless —but their situation was pretty fucking weird, and she had vulnerabilities like everyone else. She must. Despite how perfect he found her, she was only human.

"Not a happy family?" he asked.

She smirked as she walked past him into the bathroom. "God, no. But divorce is a sin, so on they trudge." She looked at him over her shoulder, rolling her eyes. "Fucking kill me now. Oh, look, there's little moisturisers in here, like a hotel."

"That's G. She takes these parties very seriously."

"She's a sweetheart," Aria said. Nik felt something in him relax, something he hadn't even realised was there. He wanted her to like his friends. He needed her to, almost.

"Eventually," Nik blurted out, "I'd like to be like my parents. Or my sister. Or even Georgia and Varo. It's ridiculous how much they love each other. That's what I want." He had no idea why he'd said that. They weren't even on that topic anymore. They'd moved on to little moisturisers, for fuck's sake, but apparently his mind hadn't gotten the message.

Still, Aria didn't question it. She leaned forward to reach the cabinet over the massive marble counter. Her top rose up, and he tried not to stare too much at the expanse of lower back it revealed. "That's funny," she said lightly. "That you're so into true love, I mean, but you've got yourself a fake girlfriend."

If only she fucking knew. "Well, I've always wanted love, but in a distant sort of way. I suppose..." He faltered as a realisation hit him. It wasn't a particularly flattering one, but he said it anyway. "I suppose I assumed it would fall into my lap, like everything else. So, I never put any effort into romance."

"Hmm." She caught his eye in the mirror. "I feel like you're expecting me to judge you here."

"Aren't you?"

"Sweetheart, I'm just trying to get paid."

He snorted, even as the words scratched at his heart. "I'm aware. So, what about you, chrysí mou?"

She smirked. "See, you think I'm gonna ask you what that means, so you can tell me some romantic shit and I'll swoon."

"Ah... What?" Nik blinked.

44

"Cut the Greek. You know it sounds sexy. And you just can't stop being a dirty little flirt." Aria winked as she strutted out of the bathroom. Her hip brushed his as she passed through the door, and Nik's mind scrambled. Did she really think Greek was sexy? And what did it mean that she'd called him *dirty* with that teasing smile on her face and that sparkle in her eyes? And why was he trying to figure out ways to get her to say it again?

Wait, what were they talking about?

Oh, yes. He hid his confusion—and his frankly excessive arousal—behind the best smirk he could muster, leaning against the doorframe with his arms folded. "You didn't answer my question. What about you?"

"About me?" She hauled her suitcase onto the bed—impressive, because that thing weighed a ton—and started the lock combination.

"Do you want to find love?"

Aria rolled her eyes. "I found it several times. Never quite got the hype. Love is like a diamond: costs a lot, has a great rep, but at the end of the day it's just a shiny rock. It has no purpose and no value beyond what we've assigned to it. Most people just want to say they've got one."

He gaped as she opened her suitcase and sorted through a pile of glittery fabrics. He had never, in all his life, heard such a cynical analysis of love. And he'd been a pro footballer since he was seventeen.

The beast she'd awoken inside him was howling its displeasure. It demanded that he prove her wrong, that he change that hard set to her pretty mouth and light up the shadows that wreathed her words. But before he could even begin, Aria looked up and flashed him a smile. "No offence," she said wryly.

Nik choked down his impassioned responses and said, "None taken."

The household staggered into life by 3 p.m. Where Nik led, Aria must follow, so she was relieved to find that his plans for the day revolved around the villa's pool. He spent the afternoon thrashing about in the water with his mates, a series of men whose names she was never going to remember. She paid attention only to the ones she'd already heard. Like Alvaro, or Varo, Nik's best friend and Georgia's boyfriend. He was a handsome Spaniard, if you were into the long-hair-and-bottomless-eyes thing. His ink was fantastic, too. And he seemed just as sweet as Georgia, if slightly quieter.

Then there was Kieran, a Brit with dark skin and a shy smile that made Aria's heart melt. She found shy people fascinating, probably because she absolutely could not relate. Whatever the reason, she liked Kieran on the spot. His girlfriend, Laurie, was less easy to warm to—not because there was anything wrong with her, but because she only spoke French. Aria had failed French at school, along with almost every other subject. She *did* manage a mangled sort of "Comment ca-va?" though. Laurie, unsurprisingly, was not particularly impressed. But they had Georgia for company on the sun loungers, nattering away non-stop and translating parts of the conversation.

"I've told everyone about you," Georgia was saying happily. "I ran through the house, I did, after youse got here! I shook all these lazy buggers awake and told 'em, Nik's got a girl!"

Thank you, Georgia, for doing half of my work for me. I can't tell you how much I appreciate it.

"Course, most of 'em fell right back to sleep." Georgia rolled her eyes. "Honestly. They best be ready to go by tonight, at least!"

"You guys take this party pretty seriously," Aria murmured, most of her attention on her sketchbook. She stared at the little

3-D heart she'd just finished shading. What should she write in the centre? *Get fucked?* Or *Dior slut?*

"You're damned right we do!" Georgia cried. "Especially the lads. Most of them don't get much time to relax."

Aria flicked a gaze over to the pool. The guys, plus a couple of girls she hadn't met yet, were playing some sort of raucous game involving three footballs and a series of highly questionable underwater tackles. "The poor dears," Aria deadpanned. "They seem *so* stressed."

Georgia snorted out a laugh. "Oh, you and Nik are so perfect for each other. I bet he absolutely dies over you! Bless him." She chuckled as if Aria and Nik pairing up was the sweetest event in modern history. Then she said something in French and Laurie started laughing too. Georgia must be some kind of linguistic genius, because earlier on she'd been speaking fluent Spanish with Alvaro. Then there was Kieran, who must speak French to date Laurie—and, of course, Nik, who spoke two languages at least.

Aria made a mental note to download DuoLingo.

"Do you fancy a bagel, babe?" Georgia asked suddenly. "I've really got a hankering, you know. Love a bagel, me."

"Oh, no thanks."

"Laurie, veux-tu un bagel?"

"Oui, merci," Laurie drawled. Aside from the movement of her bee-stung lips, the brunette remained completely still. She reminded Aria of a cat lounging on hot concrete.

As Georgia hustled off, Aria wondered if sketching Nik right now—those thick muscles dripping wet and glistening in the sun—would count as work. Because if she was his *real* girlfriend, she'd probably draw him. So, as his *fake* girlfriend...

"He-*llo*."

Aria looked up sharply at the shadowy figure looming over her. "Uh... hi?"

Talia Hibbert

The figure sat down on the sun lounger Georgia had just vacated. Now he was out of the sun, Aria saw an unusually tall man whose low-slung trunks displayed a lean, cut, tattooed body. Unfortunately, the tattoos were shit. He grinned, displaying a row of teeth that were strangely identical in size and shape, dominating his mouth like a pearly brick wall. His pale hair curled around his carved cheekbones, and his eyes were a bright, startling green.

"I've never seen *you* before," he said, leaning back on his hands in a way that sort of... puffed out his chest. He ran his eyes over her body, brows raised, and she became slightly conscious of her tiny bikini. "I'm Shenker."

Ah. There was another name she'd heard. Nik didn't like this guy. He hadn't *said* so, of course; she got the feeling he'd never say anything unkind. But when they'd been running over the endless guest list on the plane, he'd sneered slightly as he said Tom Shenker's name.

"I'm Aria," she said, offering the man a tight smile.

He gave a leisurely nod that could only be described as arrogant. "Who are you with?"

She cocked a brow, her irritation piqued. "Who says I'm *with* anyone?" But wait—that didn't sound very *I'm-so-excited-to-be-Nik's-girlfriend*, now, did it? Slapping on a smile, she added quickly, "But I am. Obviously. Just..."

Shenker's brows drew together as she stumbled over her words. Oh, fuck. This wasn't going well. *When all else fails, flirt.* Aria set her sketchbook aside and mirrored the man's posture, thrusting out her own non-existent chest. His gaze flickered, not to her tits, but down to her thighs. Good enough.

"Why don't you see if you can guess?" she asked, making her voice as breathy as it was ever gonna get. Maybe the Marilyn Monroe impression would draw attention away from her rambling mouth.

"Alright," he drawled, looking over at the pool. She followed his gaze and found the weird ball game still going strong.

Except for Nik, who stood in the middle of the watery pitch, glaring directly at them.

Oh, dear. Was she not supposed to talk to Shenker? *Oops.*

"I'm going to guess," Shenker murmured, "that it's Nik, since he's looking over here like he wants to murder me. But if you *are* with Nik, you won't be for long—"

"Charming," she snorted. "Do you often get to know people by insulting them?"

His confidence faltered a little, that odd smile slipping. "Well, I... I just meant, Nik only does casual, so if you're interested in—"

"Nik's my boyfriend, actually. And he's coming over here." *Why is he coming over here?*

Aria watched his progress with a combination of alarm and appreciation. Alarm because he had a smouldering sort of rage-y look on his face that she'd never actually seen before. Appreciation *also* because of that smouldering look, along with the droplets of water sliding down his deliciously muscular legs. Lord, the man had some *thighs*. She supposed it made sense, considering his profession, but damn.

"Boyfriend?" Shenker's expression betrayed a hint of worry, which was smart. Because, while Nik was a sweetheart with a constant smile, he also gave off this low thrum of dangerous energy, the kind that suggested he wasn't to be messed with.

And Aria, she reminded herself, was not at all attracted to that. Not in the slightest.

———

Ah, Tom Shenker. A storm cloud on a sunny day. A shit in a showroom toilet. The man was more adept at ruining Nik's mood than he was at keeping—and, Nik's hatred aside, he had to admit Shenker was a damned good keeper. The twat.

Whack—Kieran's hand landed between Nik's shoulder blades in what the short, circumspect full-back probably considered a friendly pat. "Head in the game, Christou."

Nik grunted in reply. His glower remained pinned to Aria and Shenker, chatting away on the sun loungers. Truthfully, he'd spent half the afternoon staring at Aria from the corner of his eye, anyway—she was pretty fucking easy to stare at. Especially in that shimmering string bikini, blue as the pool and tiny enough to display a body he could drown in.

Which he absolutely was not going to do, obviously.

Until she asked for it.

Suddenly, Aria and Shenker turned to look at him as one— as if they were talking about him. Ri's eyes met his, and something electric shot through his body, strong enough to snatch his breath for a second. Fuck.

"I'm going over there," he muttered, more to himself than anyone else.

Still, Kieran replied. "You don't need to worry about Shenker. That's your girl."

Wise words, except she wasn't his girl. She was just pretending to be. And while Nik knew, logically, that his fake girlfriend wasn't going to fake-cheat on him, his blood turned to ice at the thought of his very *real* obsession falling for someone else right under his nose.

That was easy enough to avoid, though. He'd just have to make sure she liked him best.

"Nik," Varo shouted. "Where you going? You're down one-nil!"

"Time out," he called over his shoulder as he hauled himself out of the pool. He could feel Aria's eyes on him, burning just like the sun-baked stone under his palms. So, he *might* have flexed a little more than necessary as he stood, and he *may* have walked over to them kind of slowly, just to enjoy the way her gaze raked over his body. And, since she was unashamedly staring, Nik decided he could do the same.

Jesus, she looked good. Sweet little tits, thick waist, hips and a belly he could grab while he fucked her. Not that he was going to fuck her. This was all just theoretical. Or rather, hopeful. She really was *covered* in tattoos, and he found himself desperate to trace every single one with his tongue—from the gemstone heart below her collarbone to the little jellyfish swimming up her ankle. She leant back against her sun lounger, one leg bent, so he caught a glimpse of the plump, bikini-covered V between her thighs.

I want that. Bad.

The need hit harder than a set of studs to the gut, almost hard enough to stop Nik in his tracks. Fuck. If he didn't stop thinking about this—about *her*—he'd be flashing his hard-on to the whole damn house in the next five minutes.

Nik tore his gaze from Aria and glared at Shenker instead, letting the man's smug-fuck face erase every last scrap of desire. Ah. Perfect.

"Shenker," he growled as he strode closer.

"Christou."

The conversation ended there. His back firmly to the other man, Nik bent by Aria's sun lounger and met her eyes. They were huge and doe-like without all the smokey makeup she preferred, tilting slightly upward at the edges. She gave him a teasing smile that set his racing heart at ease. *Obviously,* she didn't like Shenker. Nobody with any fucking sense liked Shenker—Varo just had some primary school determination to 'include everyone', so the prick was always invited to these things.

51

Talia Hibbert

In fact, Nik decided, Aria probably hated the guy. Sure, they'd only spoken for five minutes, but it was possible. In which case, she might be sitting here silently begging him to rescue her from the man's irritating presence. And Nik could never abandon a lady in distress. So he slid an arm under her bent knees, wrapped the other around her waist, and picked her up.

She sucked in a breath so hard, he was surprised she didn't choke. "What the bloody hell are you doing?" she demanded.

"You've been watching long enough, chrysí mou. Come and play." Was it his imagination, or did she shiver in his arms at that last sentence? Maybe she was cold. Somehow. In thirty-degree heat. He held her tighter just in case.

The guys in the pool cheered as Nik came closer. Aria didn't seem nearly as impressed, but he was kind of enjoying her iron grip on his biceps. He wondered if she'd dig her fingers into his skin like that when she came on his cock.

If she came on his cock. Which she might never do, if he fucked this week up.

"This is a health and safety hazard," she said, her voice dry as ever. "You're about to slip, drop me, land on your arse and crack both our heads open."

"I can assure you, my motor skills are better than that."

"Isn't your knee fucked up?"

"It's still stronger than the average knee." According to his physio, anyway.

"Sounds like bullshit," she sang. He liked the smile on her face, liked the sight of her eyes sparkling in the sunlight and the way she tapped her tongue against her lip ring. Her navel was pierced too, twice. He didn't even know you *could* pierce it twice.

He wondered if she'd pierced anything else.

"Throw her in!" Varo shouted. Everyone in the pool

52

cheered, and the shout caught on. "Throw her in! Throw her in!"

"Don't you fucking dare," Aria whispered. And then, almost immediately, she winced. She must realise, then, that she'd said exactly the wrong thing.

Nik's grin widened. "But sweetheart, I want to get you wet."

"Oh, you filthy fuck—*ooh!*" she half-screamed as he started running, escalating to a full-on screech when he jumped into the pool, carrying her with him. As they plunged in, Nik pushed her up, so her head wouldn't be submerged. He doubted she'd remembered to hold her breath in between screaming *"You absolute prick!"* Plus, he had a feeling that she might punch him if he got her hair wet.

The water felt ice-cold against his sun-warmed skin. When Nik's feet hit the bottom of the pool, he pushed up and broke the surface again, sending a spray of water arcing through the air. He shook his head like a dog and grinned in the face of her death-glare. "What? You don't want to swim?"

"For all you know, I *can't* swim!"

He slid his arm around her waist, pulling her back against his chest. "You don't need to swim. I've got you."

"Oh, bugger off," she muttered. But her hand rose to slide over his jaw. She turned her head and kissed his cheek. It was that kiss, combined with her soft arse pressing against him below the water, that sent every drop of blood in Nik's body rushing to his dick. He was hard as a fucking rock, *painfully* hard, within seconds. And he saw the instant Aria felt it, because her smile faded, and her eyes flashed up to his, wide and questioning.

He froze. They hadn't discussed this, because he hadn't expected this. He wasn't some kind of depraved sex pest. Regardless of his hopes, he had not foreseen a situation where he ended up rubbing his erection all over Aria in front of about twenty people. And because of those twenty people, he now had to let go of her in a way that wouldn't seem suspicious.

Or at least, he thought he did. Until she reached up and kissed him.

Because his friends were all five years old, a cheer went up the minute her lips touched his. Fireworks would have been more appropriate, because for the second time in his life, Nik was absolutely undone by a kiss. It was the way she arched her back, pressing her arse harder against his cock, and the gentle tug as she sucked his lower lip into her mouth. When the tip of her tongue teased his, Nik actually moaned. He wanted to shove down his trunks, slide her bikini aside and thrust his aching—

"Heads!" Varo shouted. One of the three footballs in play plopped into the water beside them, sending up a huge splash. Aria broke the kiss with a laugh, as if it was that easy. As if she could go from that impossible heat and uncontrollable need to carefree playfulness within seconds.

Which, clearly, she could. But Nik, for the first time in his life, was struggling to do the same.

She pulled the ball closer with her fingertips and shouted to Varo, "What am I supposed to do with this?"

"You're on my team," he grinned. "Bring it over here."

"She's on *my* team," Nik managed to growl.

"Too late," Aria teased, her tone sing-song. "Sorry, love." She leaned in to kiss his cheek and whispered in his ear, "How am I doing?"

Then, as reality filtered in—as he remembered that she wasn't his, that the kiss hadn't been real at all—she winked and swam away.

Chapter 4

Make It Tequila

There wasn't a single clock in Varo's huge, fancy house. Aria knew, because when the sun hung low in the sky and her lungs were exhausted with laughing and swimming, she'd excused herself to wander through the villa's cool, cavernous halls.

The place was like a magical world; timeless, unbelievably luxurious, and oddly silent—except for the chatter of the cleaners, who flitted in and out of rooms like fairies.

But the disorientating bubble of the villa didn't faze the industrious Georgia. It was around 6 p.m., according to Aria's phone, when the little bombshell—a word that described her in every possible way—began running through the house, ordering everyone to get ready. "We're going out! No, don't moan, Kieran; it's just a light one tonight. Dinner! A bar or five! It'll be fun!"

One of the guys whose names Aria refused to remember wandered into the room, dripping wet, a phone pressed to his ear. "Sí. Sí, queremos—wait, hold on a sec. Hey. Yo, Nik's girl."

Aria looked up from her own phone, pasting a smile on her

face. Her thumbs kept moving as she tapped out an outraged text to Jen.

> Everyone keeps calling me Nik's FUCKING girl!

"Yeah?"

"You want some blow?"

She narrowly avoided gawping like a cartoon character. And only because she had decades of experience in being cool as shit. "Um... nah. No thanks, man. I'm good."

"Cool, cool." The guy switched back to Spanish and disappeared.

What the hell kind of people just... ordered their cocaine by phone? Like it was a bloody Chinese takeaway? Rich people, she supposed.

"Aria!" Georgia shrieked, barrelling back into the room. "Get ready! We're leaving in four hours!"

"Am I... supposed to take four hours to—?"

Georgia slapped her hands against the cushions either side of Aria's head and leaned in, her expression grim. "Time is different here," she whispered darkly. "It'll take you forty minutes just to get your falsies on."

Aria didn't mention the fact that it took her forty minutes on a good day. False eyelashes were not her area of expertise. "Oh, right. Okay then."

"Chop chop!" Georgia cried, already running off through the house. "Let's go, people! Let's go! Where's Varo? Varo, pon tu trasero aquí, you tit!"

Three hours later, Aria realised that Georgia hadn't been exaggerating. She'd never taken this long to get ready in her life.

She rifled through her makeup bag for some lip gloss and ran through a mental checklist. Dress: present and correct, the low-cut neckline secured with acres of tit tape. Shoes: by the bed, just waiting to be worn. Jewellery: her bracelets were fine, her necklace was fine, but she might change the studs in her earlobes for some hoops...

She barely registered the fact that the shower's distant splash, audible through the bathroom door, had stopped. But she sure as shit noticed a second later when that door opened to reveal Nik, his tawny skin glistening, his gorgeous body barely covered by the little white towel slung low on his hips.

Aria stared at his reflection in the mirror, her mouth suddenly dry, her heart pounding. Despite herself, she squeezed her thighs together under the dressing table, a spark of heat flicking to life in her belly. Baby Jesus on a cracker, he was so damn fine. He raised an arm to scratch his head, revealing that even his fucking armpit hair was sexy. How could armpit hair be sexy? Was she high?

No, just horny. Basically, the same thing.

Nik's absent gaze found hers in the mirror, and his distracted expression disappeared. He was all focus now, dark eyes sharpening, that wide mouth tilting into a smirk. Probably because she was staring so hard.

"Close your mouth," he winked, "before you catch something."

Aria dropped her lip gloss. Oops. "Piss off."

"Just some friendly advice." The lip gloss rolled toward him, and he bent to pick it up. Call her a perverted motherfucker, because Aria watched eagerly for some slippage in that towel. It was just plain curiosity, that's all. She'd never been with a guy who had thighs like fucking tree trunks. She wanted to know if they made his dick look smaller by comparison.

Though it certainly hadn't *felt* small, earlier in the pool.

Nik picked up the lip gloss—his towel remaining tragically secure—and moved closer to the vanity. But he didn't hand it over. Instead, he squatted down beside her chair, those muscular thighs and solid calves making her mouth water. Aria's gaze caught on the way his towel rode up, and then on the carved lines of his abdomen, and then on the little drops of water sliding through his chest hair. Finally, she reached his face and found him smirking.

"You look good," he said.

"You don't have to compliment me, Nik. That's not in the contract."

"I know. But since my eyes are working fine, and I can speak, and you're wearing *that*... I might as well tell you. You look good." His gaze ran from her bare legs to the low V of her neckline. He reached out and traced a finger over the fine cross tattooed between her breasts. She tried not shiver as his calloused skin rasped over hers. Her nipples felt like bullets, so sensitive she almost whimpered as they tightened against her dress.

For a moment, his gaze held hers, hot and dark with promise. But then he looked away, shaking his head slightly, breaking the contact between them.

"Sorry," he said, holding out the lip gloss. "I meant to take my clothes into the bathroom. I forgot."

The loaded meaning behind that apology stiffened her spine. "It really doesn't matter to me."

Nik arched a brow. "It doesn't matter to you if I wander around half-naked?"

"Nope." His fingers brushed hers as he handed the little tube of gloss over, and the heat stirring between her thighs became a full-blown inferno. She was surprised she didn't burst into flames. Still, she opened the lip gloss and prayed her hands

The Fake Boyfriend Fiasco

wouldn't shake as she applied it. The way her heart was pounding, they just might.

"Are you sure? Because it seems like it does."

Well, that did it. Pride and stubbornness truly piqued, Aria turned a slow, disgusted look at him. "Sweetheart. Do you know how many men I've seen naked?"

His smirk faded at that, becoming something slightly darker. "I could not *begin* to guess."

"Enough. More than enough, really. You could walk around swinging your dick like a toddler, and I wouldn't bat an eyelash. So, don't ever think I'm concerned by your abs and your... towel." Her don't-fuck-with-me tone might have faltered a little bit at the end, there. But he didn't seem to notice; he was too busy scowling at her, his usually cheerful face thunderous.

"So, you don't care," he said flatly, "if I wander around naked. You are not remotely affected by my presence."

She rolled her eyes, flicking her hair as she turned back to the mirror. "Feel free to strip off and stick this lip gloss up your arse, if you want. I've got plenty more."

He straightened up abruptly. "That's great. Since you don't mind, I'll just behave as I usually would." And then he dropped the towel.

She absolutely did not look. Not at all. And he certainly didn't stand there and shove it in her face. No, he turned away almost immediately, casually going about his business. He got dressed while telling her where they were going for dinner, how much Varo and Kieran liked her, and complimenting her overhead throw.

While Aria applied her bloody lip gloss, and hummed in response, and acted natural. And tried not to think about the glimpse she'd gotten from the corner of her eye, just before he'd turned away. A glimpse of his thick, dark cock, not hanging by his thigh, but standing hard against his stomach.

Only she couldn't *stop* thinking about it. Oh, dear.

"I think I've found my people," Aria shouted over the music, leaning against the bar. "Cuz if this is your friends' idea of a quiet night..."

Nik knocked back another shot and grinned through the harsh taste. "It was *supposed* to be a quiet night. But sometimes we get carried away."

She laughed a little louder than usual, throwing her head back. The movement made her wobble on her high heels, so he wrapped a hand around her upper arm to hold her steady.

"I think I might actually be *drunk*," she said, finally figuring out what her bright eyes had already told him.

"I'd fucking hope so after all that vodka."

She scoffed. "Clearly, I'm not used to shots that aren't cheap and watered down. You can let go now."

Nik wet his lips, feeling slightly dizzy himself. It wasn't alcohol, though—at least, not all of it. Hours of drinking with Aria, dancing with Aria, trying and failing not to flirt with Aria, were going to his head way faster than the booze. And the silken feel of her skin against his palm wasn't helping. "Right," he nodded. "Of course. Yeah."

She looked down at his hand, which hadn't moved. Then she looked up at him. He thought she was trying to arch a brow, but it came out more like a surprised-looking head loll. "Nik—"

"Sorry." He dragged his hand away and slapped it on the bar, letting the cool chrome soothe his skin. He felt like he was burning. Maybe he really was drunk. Because he was *supposed* to be getting to know her, not mauling her like a twat.

"You know, you're really cute," she said. "Sometimes, I mean. Other times you're kind of scary-sexy."

He frowned, biting the inside of his cheek. "I scare you?" That was the last thing he'd wanted. But he knew he pushed things too far, sometimes—all the time, actually—and Aria, tough as she seemed, was fragile if you took a minute to look. "I'm sorry. I'm really sorry, Ri."

"No, no, you don't scare me. I mean, you don't *scare* me, scare me. It's more like... you know when you're about to do a guy and he whips out some monster dick and you're like, *Well, fuck, how's that gonna fit?*"

A smile tugged at his lips. "No, I don't know. I usually—"

"Nope!" She held up a hand. "No more filth from you, sir! Not when you make it sound so good."

His smile blossomed into a grin. "Good, huh?" Nik leaned in close, smoothing her hair out of her face. This time, he knew he didn't imagine her shiver, the way she shifted restlessly as his fingers skimmed her neck. He brought his lips close to her ear and asked, "You like my dirty mouth, moro mou?"

She met his gaze, her glossy lips parted. Every time she reapplied that fucking lip gloss tonight, he remembered the way she'd looked at him earlier in their room. She thought his mouth was filthy, but she'd die if she heard him thinking about what else would make those lips shine.

"Maybe I do," she said finally.

"Would you like to hear more?"

One of Aria's many wonderful traits, he was learning, was the fact that she never backed down. If he was outrageous, she outdid him. If he laid down a gauntlet, she picked it up. So, he was awaiting her response with almost embarrassing eagerness when he felt a strange hand sliding up his arm, demanding his attention.

Turning to glare at the owner of that hand, Nik snapped, "*What?*"

A redhead with cheekbones sharper than a knife blinked up

61

at him. "Aren't you Nikolas Christou?" she asked, excitement all over her face.

Well, now he felt bad, snarling at a fan. With a sigh, Nik drummed up a weak smile and nodded. "Yep. That's me."

"Oh my God!" She leaned in, her hand sliding further up his arm—okay, so she was touchy—over his shoulder—friendly, then—and down his chest...

Until Aria grabbed the girl's wrist between finger and thumb like it was a bag of dog shit, pushing it away. "He's busy," she drawled, running her own hand through Nik's hair. There was a possessive edge to her touch that made his muscles tighten and his blood race.

The redhead gave Aria a look that was half-nervous, half-disgusted, and 100% pissing Nik off. "Calm down. I'm just trying to talk to him—"

"Talk less. Walk more."

After a moment's tense hesitation, the woman turned with a huff and a flick of bright hair. Aria watched her go with clear amusement, shaking her head slowly. Then she turned back to the bar. "That's another shot for you, sugar."

He should never have agreed to this game. He hadn't realised before, but it seemed like he actually *did* need Aria—and not just because her presence soothed all his niggling anxieties. He'd been approached by more than enough people tonight to warrant a fake-girlfriend-bodyguard. So many, in fact, that she'd turned it into a drinking game.

He wrinkled his nose at the prospect of more alcohol. He was going to end up getting his stomach pumped. "Oh, come on. She was barely flirting."

Aria snorted. "After tonight, I'm starting to understand why you hired me. That was a blatant come-on. No wonder you fall into bed with people and don't even know how it happened." She raised a hand to catch the bartender's attention.

"You're trying to kill me, aren't you? That's what this is about."

"You're not backing down, are you? We agreed. A shot for everyone I get rid of."

"Fine," Nik sighed. "Make it tequila, this time."

"You guys want to stay up and smoke?"

Aria paused in the act of unbuckling her shoe, leaning drunkenly against the hallway wall. She looked up at Varo with her mouth hanging open, shock overtaking the ache in her feet. "You can't be serious."

No-one heard her over the sound of enthusiastic agreement. Apparently, this group of absolute nightmares weren't ready for bed yet. How, she had no idea.

Nik appeared by her side, keeping her steady with an arm around her waist. "Relax," he murmured. "I'm taking you to bed."

The words zipped through her like electricity. *Down, girl. He didn't mean it like that.* "We can stay up, if you'd like."

He chuckled. "Please. I saw your face just now. There's no way I'm getting between you and sleep. Anyway, I'm tired too."

"Well, in that case..." She straightened up, holding her shoes, and wiggled her poor toes against the cold floor. "Ahhh, that's good."

"Give me those." He took the shoes in one hand and twined their fingers together with the other. He'd been holding her hand all night, pulling her here and there. She found herself wondering—was Nik this affectionate with everyone? Judging by the awed looks his friends were giving her, apparently not. But if he were in a real relationship, would he be?

She remembered what he'd said before, about wanting love.

About his parents, and his sister's marriage. Yeah, she decided. He'd be like this in a relationship.

It was worrying how much the thought appealed to her.

"We're gonna head upstairs," Nik called as they walked away. "See you all tomorrow."

There were a variety of responses, from Kieran's *Later, guys*, to Georgia's *Bye, hon!* to the low, ribald mutterings of some of the men.

"I'd take her to bed, and all!" shouted a pink-faced blond named Harry with laughter in his voice.

Aria rolled her eyes. "Your friends are children," she murmured as they reached the stairs.

Nik flashed her a sleepy grin. "That's why we get on so well."

Aria stood in front of the enormous bathroom mirror, biting her lip as she stared at her reflection. She usually slept naked, but she'd brought pyjamas along for this trip, for obvious reasons. The little vest top was fine, even if it did cling to her belly for dear life—but the bottoms turned out to be way too hot, even with the air con blasting. So, she was standing there in her vest and the biggest pair of knickers she owned—which weren't that big—wondering if it would be incredibly weird to lie next to Nik in bed like this.

I bet he won't be wearing pyjamas.

True.

It's not that different from a bikini. In fact, you're showing less skin than you were by the pool.

Also true.

He was wandering around bare-arsed in front of you six

hours ago. You really don't need to consider his delicate sensibilities.

Okay, that decided the matter. He'd take her knickers and he'd fucking like it.

"Wow. That thought came out much dirtier than intended." She shook her head at herself in the mirror and turned to leave the bathroom.

Nik was already in bed, the sheets pushed down enough to show his bare chest and the arrow of hair above his waistband. He was in his underwear, then. She hoped he was, anyway, because otherwise he must be bloody naked.

Still, she felt a little awkward as his eyes tracked her path from the bathroom to the bed. He didn't say a word, which wasn't like him. It wasn't like him at all. And maybe it was the alcohol in her system, but this silence was making her nervous.

"So," she said brightly as she climbed into bed. "How—oh, holy shit, this mattress is amazing."

"Yeah," he agreed. That was it. Just, *Yeah.* His voice was soft, almost raspy, and his gaze never left her, even as she laid down beside him.

Aria cleared her throat. "Um, anyway... How do you think today went?"

"It was good." He turned on his side to face her, and God, this was just too much. His golden skin and dark stubble against the white pillow, his brown eyes turning onyx in the shadows, the way his voice lowered almost intimately. It hit Aria all at once that *she was in bed with Nik.* They'd expected this, discussed it, agreed to it—but she was starting to realise she hadn't been ready for it. Plans had nothing on actually being with him.

Pretending to be with him, she reminded herself sharply. Pretending. *You can't be with* anyone. *You've proven that much.*

And when a contract is involved, it's best to keep your thoughts compartmentalised.

That's what she needed to do, Aria decided. Yes, she was attracted to Nik, and yes, she liked Nik, and yes, she was in bed with Nik. And all of that was fine, as long as she compartmentalised.

"What do you think?" he asked suddenly. "Was it good for you?"

She didn't miss his teasing inflection or the slight curve of his lush lips.

"Oh, it was great for me," she purred, just to watch that little smile of his turn into a grin. He didn't disappoint, his eyes lighting up the way they always did when she took his shit and gave it right back. "By the way, thanks for not getting my hair wet in the pool."

He laughed. "You noticed that?"

"Of course I noticed. It was kind of impressive, actually. But this is a sew-in. You can get it wet. I mean, I'd rather you didn't, but I won't throttle you if you do."

"Ah," he grinned, tapping her on the nose. "You might regret telling me that."

She scoffed to hide the fact that a single nose tap had turned her mind all rosy and fizzy like pink champagne.

"Now, I was going to ask this in the morning," he went on, "but I suppose it is morning now, and we're talking, so." He shrugged, and his shoulder brushed hers ever so slightly. After a night of dancing with him, holding his hand, and hanging off his arm whenever admirers got too close, the touch should've felt like nothing.

Should've.

"If there are any boundaries that you want to shift," he said, "let me know. I mean, anything we've discussed that you want to change now. Like the touching."

She blinked, surprise corralling her scattered thoughts. "You'd be willing to change things now, after we've already started?"

"I don't want you to be uncomfortable. I thought I should check in. And I wanted to tell you: if I'm ever out of line, don't think you can't stop me just because everyone's watching. Just tell me to fuck off. I mean, that's what you'd do if you were really my girlfriend." He paused for a moment, looking thoughtful. "But if you don't want to do that, we could have a... a safe word, for when we're in public. Something you can work into conversation, to let me know if I'm doing shit you don't like." He finished that baffling speech with a sweet little smile that, if Aria wasn't mistaken, was supposed to reassure her.

She wasn't reassured. Well, she *was* sure that Nik meant everything he said. His consideration was genuine—but all that did was make her worry, because he was so fucking sweet. Sweet enough to ruin all the little boxes she'd stored her neatly wrapped-up emotions in. Aria knew she'd grown up starved of affection, knew she inhaled love like it was oxygen, knew that all too often she gulped down toxic, poisoned air in her quest for a connection. But despite all that—and despite knowing how badly she'd fucked up last time—the hole in her chest had started to whisper that surely *this* man would be the one to fill her up.

No. No. This man is not for us.

"I'll remember that," she said finally. "Thank you. And as far as the safe word goes..." She ignored, with difficulty, the sexual implications of that phrase. This was business, dammit. "I'm thinking banana split."

"Banana split?"

"Yep. But, really, so far, I'm fine with how things are between us." *So, so fine. Almost as fine as your perfect fucking face.*

Nik's smile was soft and pleased, his happiness glowing like the bedside lamp behind him. "Good." Then he reached out and ran the tip of one blunt finger over her lower lip—over her lip ring, she realised. He didn't seem seductive; just curious. Which was galling, because that small touch had her nipples tightening within seconds. If he looked down, he'd see them poking holes through her vest.

Please don't look down.

"You can really hold your liquor," he said, pulling his finger away.

"Yeah," she managed. "Of course I can. I'm British."

He grinned. "I like that." Then he rose up on one elbow, his biceps bulging right in front of her face as he reached over for the lamp switch. "We should really sleep, shouldn't we? You ready?"

"I'm ready."

The light winked out. "Night."

How can this thing between us feel like more of a connection than every relationship I've ever had? How can an acquaintance and a few fake kisses be more solid than any ephemeral love I've chased? Why does everyone else taste like crappy corner shop sweets in my memory, but you taste like brown sugar melting on my tongue?

"Night," she said.

And lay there in the dark, burning, burning, burning.

Chapter 5

Lay It Like a Chicken

Nik had been hoping that Aria snored.

He doubted it would turn him off, because she was just—God, she was incredibly fucking hot. But if she snored, it might've been easier to get irritated with her. To think something like, *Damn, I can't wait for this week to end so I can sleep without her snoring in my ear.* Unfortunately, she wouldn't allow him even that small solace. Aria didn't snore, or drool, or kick him in her sleep. Nothing.

He watched her in the faint light that crept past their closed curtains. She slept on her stomach, spread out like a starfish, and he slept on his back, also spread out like a starfish. So, he'd woken to find his right limbs tangled with hers, her skin almost feverish. They'd somehow thrown off the sheets, so the first thing Nik saw when he woke up that morning was Aria's tight, lacy underwear, barely big enough to cover her arse. No tattoos there. He'd noticed that the day before, but the knowledge felt different now.

Maybe because the second thing he'd seen when he woke up was her face. Her cheeks, soft and smushed and lined with pillow creases; her long eyelashes and the shadows of left-over makeup under her eyes; her slightly parted lips, moving as she breathed deeply. When he looked at her, he'd been seized by the urge to kiss those lips. Thank God he'd come to his senses a moment later. He was trying to make her like him, not assault her while she slept.

Nik sighed and stared up at the ceiling, pressing a hand against his aching cock. He was so hard; his morning piss was about to be a fucking nightmare—but he wasn't focusing on that right now. He was more concerned with how weird last night had been. He hadn't considered how different it would feel, going out with a girlfriend instead of just his mates. Different, but good. Their relationship might be fake, but the way he'd felt —as if she were his sun, and he'd spent the whole night orbiting her? That had been real.

Real, and painfully natural. Checking on her, making sure she had a drink, watching her laugh and dance with Georgia; none of that had been a chore. And since Nik knew he was a self-absorbed bastard, that fact struck him as... interesting. Honestly, he adored her. And he was convinced, by this point, that she at least wanted him. Not in the plastic, automatic way most people wanted him, for his looks or his money, but in a way that felt personal. So fucking personal. He'd slept with countless people, but he only felt desired when she looked at him.

Those looks didn't do shit to soothe the demanding hunger inside him, though. In fact, they made things worse. Because she still wasn't his, and the idea that maybe she *could* be was like dangling meat in front of a wolf. Stifling a groan, Nik eased out of bed and headed for the shower. He stood under its powerful spray seconds later, tipping his head back as if the water could wash away his confusion.

It didn't. He was still hopelessly attached, ridiculously horny, and as reckless as ever. He was also carrying out a plan so far-fetched and audacious, he could barely believe his own gall.

He could only deal with one of those issues, though, so he set the rest aside and focused on his throbbing cock.

His hands slick with soap, Nik bowed his head beneath the shower's spray and slid a fist over his aching length. *Oh, fuck. Yes.* He stroked himself hard. Harder. Imagined that the tight, wet glide of his fist was Aria's mouth, because if he let himself think about her pussy, he'd really be fucked.

He'd meant to stay quiet, but as he envisioned Aria on her knees before him, he moaned. His strokes sped up, his grip tightening, desire licking at him like hot flames. And then he imaged her pulling back, running the swollen head of his cock over her lips, slicking them with his pre-come the way she'd slicked them with gloss last night...

He grunted as the wave of pleasure broke too early, his come spilling hot into his hand. "Shit." He shouldn't have done that. Even as his body tingled with barely-sated arousal, he knew: he shouldn't have fucking done that. Because now he'd really let himself imagine it, he'd never be free of those mental images. Not unless he got his hands on her—and he still didn't know if he ever would.

The spark between them could just reflect his own desire. He could be imagining everything he thought he'd seen in her eyes. He was starving for her, and every sarcastic comment she threw, every arched brow and unspoken challenge, made it a thousand times worse. And he loved it.

Water ran into Nik's eyes as he stared at the come painting his palm. His cock was already hardening again. He was acting like a teenager. But when he was with her, he wanted more than ever to be a man.

By that afternoon, the sun was beating down as if it wanted to kill them all.

They should probably go inside, but a few of them had started messing around with a football, and now they'd never stop. There was nothing better than a kick-about, in Nik's book. Especially when it was like this: barefoot on the grass, the ball making a satisfying *thwack* against his skin with each leisurely pass, his two best mates laughing and chatting with him.

And his woman in sight, wearing one of those tiny bikinis, that ever-present sketchbook in her hands.

Not your woman, said the voice of reason.

She should be, said the voice of every reckless thing Nik had ever done.

Really, that voice hadn't steered him wrong yet. He should probably be alarmed by how attached he was after a chance meeting, a handful of kisses, several obnoxious emails and a couple days of faking it. But, technically, Nik had known Aria for weeks now. If they were his parents, they'd already be married.

The ball hit him squarely in the thigh, bringing Nik back to the game with a jolt.

"Stop thinking about your girlfriend." Varo grinned.

Nik snorted as he passed back. "You're always thinking about yours."

"Quietly, though. When you've got Aria on your mind, your thoughts might as well be a foghorn."

Kieran chuckled. "He's not wrong. You really like this girl."

"I do. I really fucking do." It wasn't a lie, but an admission. It occurred to him that despite the secrecy around he and Aria, he could still ask his friends for advice about this. "Guys, how do you figure out... you know, feelings?"

The other men paused, the ball forgotten between them.

They shared a look, their faces unreadable. And then, as if on cue, they both burst into laughter.

"What?" Nik demanded. "This is serious! I am ignorant! Help me!"

"Dios mio," Varo wheezed, slapping his thigh—which, frankly, Nik thought was a bit much. "Oh, Nik. I really don't know what to do with you."

"I don't know how you managed to catch her in the first place," Kieran chuckled. "You're so shit at this stuff."

"I *know* I'm shit at this stuff," Nik said. "I have no idea what I'm doing. I think I might—" he broke off, astonished at the words that had almost come out of his mouth. *I think I might love her.*

Actually, that would make a lot of sense. But he'd think about it later.

Correcting himself smoothly, Nik said, "I'm not sure if she likes me as much as I like her."

Varo shrugged. "Probably not."

"Thanks for the support."

"I'm just saying! She's too cool for you." Varo dodged, laughing, as Nik kicked the ball toward his head. "Alright, calm down. She likes you. Of course, she likes you. Anyone can see that."

The words mollified Nik a little. *Anyone* could see it? So, it wasn't just a figment of his desperate imagination.

"I do have some advice, though," Kieran piped up. "I know you don't think it's a big deal, so you probably haven't told her. But trust me, people care about this kind of thing when they're in relationships."

"What?" The ball rolled back to Nik, and he tapped it neatly at Varo.

"You should probably mention that you fucked Laurie. And G. And Varo. And Tom—"

"Okay, yeah," Nik interrupted. "I get it."

Aria already knew about Tom. She knew about everyone he'd slept with in this house—except his friends, because she hadn't needed to know. They weren't on his *I regret it, steer clear* list. They were on his *That was fun* list, or in Varo and G's case, his *Let's do this again some time* list. Would Aria care? Honestly, he wasn't sure.

"You're right." Nik nodded. "I'll tell her."

"I can't believe you haven't already." Varo grinned. "How the hell did you get a girlfriend, again?"

I paid.

"Speaking of..." Kieran's dark gaze shifted to the right, his brows raising as he trailed off.

Nik looked over to find fucking Shenker looming over Aria, Laurie and G like a vulture. The slimy piece of shit. What part of *That's my only, solo, monogamous fucking girlfriend* did that prick not understand?

"Woah, man," Varo said quietly. "Relax."

Which was when Nik realised he was clenching his fists hard enough to make his knuckles ache. He took a deep breath and released the tight grip, ignoring his friends' stares. Nik rarely lost his temper—only on the pitch, and even then, it took a lot of fucking provocation. His mates would be wondering what the hell was wrong with him. They didn't know how much he really hated Shenker, because Nik didn't have the energy to talk shit.

"I don't want him bothering her," he said flatly.

"Okaaaay..." Varo replied. "*Is* he bothering her? I know Shenker's a flirt, but I've never heard about him crossing the line."

"I don't know. I just don't fucking like it." His eyes settled on the ball at his feet, and an idea winked into his brain like a lightbulb.

"Nik," Varo said slowly. "Whatever you're about to do..."

Nik ignored him, moving back a few spaces to give himself a run-up.

"At least let Varo take it," Kieran sighed. "He's the striker."

"You think I can't hit him?" Nik asked.

Varo rolled his eyes at Kieran. "Now you've done it."

"Bet me."

"Nik," Kieran scoffed, "we're not placing bets on this juvenile—"

"5000 Euro," Varo interrupted. "Ten if you get his head."

"Done. Kieran?"

There was a long pause, followed by a deep sigh. "I'm in."

Nik grinned. Then he hoofed it.

The ball arced through the air so beautifully, he almost came. Christ, that was a perfect feeling. But not as perfect as the laughter that ripped from him when the ball smacked Shenker squarely in the back the head.

Shenker staggered, caught his balance, clutched his head, and spun. "What the fuck?" he bellowed.

"Sorry, man," Nik shouted. "Thought you'd catch it." Beside him, Varo dissolved into peals of laughter.

And so, did Aria, metres away, her hand slapped over her mouth and her eyes bright.

The boys messed around with that football for hours—long enough that Aria should've been bored or irritated by the afternoon sun. But when her mind wandered from the contents of her sketchbook it found plenty of entertainment in watching Nik. He was shirtless and barefoot, running around the grass with a focus that was somehow turning her on. When beads of sweat slid down her spine, she imagined the same moisture caressing Nik's skin. When they rolled between her breasts, she imagined his tongue licking them off.

Fuck. She felt like she'd been permanently wet for the past two days. Aria was surprised she hadn't started walking funny, her clit felt so swollen and sensitive. If she didn't do something about this, she'd end up losing her head. She could barely think straight.

Which was concerning, really. After all, she *was* at work. Concentration seemed vital in her position. Which made it her professional duty to handle the throbbing pulse of desire that had taken over her body. Right?

Right.

Aria stood, picking up her sketchbook. "Sorry, guys, but I'm going to head upstairs. I think I've had too much sun."

"Oh, no, babe." Georgia leapt up and pressed a hand to Aria's brow, even though she practically had to jump to reach. "Are you alright? Do you want me to come with you?"

"No, no! I'm fine. I'm just going to rest."

"Shall I tell Nik?"

"God, no. Honestly, I'm fine. I'll just have a little sleep before we head out."

"Alright then, love," Georgia allowed, with one last worried look.

"Au revoir," Laurie murmured airily, calm and catlike as ever.

Aria hurried off into the house.

She climbed the first flight of stairs steadily. On the second flight, her steps became a slight jog, and by the third and final one, she was practically running. She rushed into the bedroom and shut the door behind her, shivering and feverish all at once. Electric anticipation rolled through her as she hauled her suitcase out of the wardrobe and pulled out the sleek black box where she'd stored anything sex-related ever since her awkward teenage years.

The sox's contents had changed a little since then. There were condoms, lube, the usual—but now she had an impressive collection of toys, too. And since she'd been purposefully, painfully celibate for months now—since November—those were the stars of her show. She put the sox down at the foot of the bed and studied its treasures, the sweet-sharp ache between her thighs worsening which each second. Finally, she pulled out a purple Rampant Rabbit, tracing a finger over the long curve of the dildo, then the 'ears' attached to its shaft, designed to vibrate against her clit.

She was already wet, but she rifled through the box for some lube anyway; there was no such thing as *too* wet, after all. She caught sight of a little bottle lurking under her butt plugs.

Then the bedroom door opened.

Shit, shit, shit.

The vibrator landed back in its box with an ominous *thunk* as shock loosened Aria's fingers.

Nik stood in the doorway, looking pretty fucking surprised himself. "Georgia said you..." He frowned, stepping into the room, shutting the door behind him. "What are you doing?"

"Nothing!" she said brightly, looking around for the sox's lid. Where the fuck had she put that thing?

"Aria." Nik's tone was calm and steady as he came closer. "What is that?"

Well, there was really nothing for it. Slapping a smile on her face, Aria turned around and sat on the box of toys. She just... sat. There was a hideous *creak*, and she felt the poor thing give under her enormous arse, but she kept her smile firmly in place. "What's what?"

Nik's lips twitched with the effort of holding back his laughter. "The thing you just sat on."

"I don't know what you're talking about," she said primly.

He studied her awkward perch on the bed, clearly skeptical. "Get up, then."

"No, thank you," she clipped out. "I'm not feeling very well."

All at once, concern softened his features. Nik sank to his knees in front of her, then winced.

"Are you supposed to do that?" she asked, remembering the recurring injury that he *claimed* was just fine. It probably wasn't quite so fine after he'd spent all day playing football.

"Doesn't matter. Are you okay? Georgia said you felt weird." He smoothed a hand over her hair like she was a fucking kitten or something. "Do you want a drink? Are you hungry?"

Well, now she felt bad. He actually seemed worried. "Um, no. No, I just need a rest."

Nik nodded slowly. "Why don't you lie down?"

"I will." Her voice came out a bit too high and squeaky.

He arched a brow, suspicion creeping into his gaze again. "Okay."

There was a pause. Apparently, he was waiting for her to move. Aria, meanwhile, was trying to figure out how to make a box of dildos disappear. Why had she even brought the fucking thing?

Oh, yes; because she was incredibly horny at the best of times, and he was gorgeous enough to make the issue almost unbearable.

"Aria," he said, "what is that?"

"What is *what*?" she snapped. He couldn't see the sox she was currently crushing to death, could he?

No; Nik's gaze wasn't even close to her arse. He was staring at the suitcase she'd dragged out of the wardrobe—or rather, at the lid of the sox, sitting beside it on the cream carpet.

"Oh," she said quickly, "that. It's... nothing."

His smile turned predatory, a cocky glint lighting his eyes. She could tell just by the look on his face that he was taking this interaction as a challenge.

Which did not bode well for her.

"Nothing?" he repeated. "So, it's definitely not the lid of the box you just sat on?"

"I'm not sitting on anything," she said stiffly.

"You're not?"

"No! Good Lord. *Sitting...* on a *box...* why would I possibly do such a thing?"

"Sweetheart. Move, or I will move you."

"Fuck off," she scowled. "You can't—" Aria broke off as she remembered that, yes, he could. He'd already proven he was strong enough to throw her around. Fuck. "You put a hand on me, and I'll bite you."

Grinning, he leaned in until their noses *almost* touched. "Don't tease, moro mou."

"Nik..."

"If you want to bite me, you can. You only ever had to ask." She became uncomfortably aware of the fact that he was only wearing a pair of swimming trunks, his chest bare. And she was only wearing a bikini, for that matter. A bikini whose top he was now staring at openly, because her nipples were hard enough to cut diamonds. They only got harder when he released a low, heavy breath that almost sounded like a moan, dragging his teeth over his lower lip.

"I should warn you," he murmured, his voice rough. "I bite back."

"Menstrual cups!" she blurted out.

Nik looked up with a blink. "What?"

Yes, Aria. What?

"Um... In the box." Her words blurred together awkwardly. Her heart felt like it might burst out of her chest and flop

Talia Hibbert

around on the floor like a fish. How the fuck could one man be so disarmingly, stressfully sexy? "My menstrual cups," she repeated, "are in the box."

He paused. Then, rather than blushing, or stuttering, or—the ideal scenario—*leaving the room*, Nik said, "The box you supposedly are not sitting on."

She sighed. "Obviously, I'm sitting on a fucking box, Nik. And the corners are starting to hurt, so if you could just piss off—"

"What," he cut in casually, "is a menstrual cup?"

Oh, dear. She really hadn't thought this through. Good thing she refused to be embarrassed about good, old-fashioned menstruation. "Well, it's a little silicone cup thing that you kind of... fold up, and shove up your vagina—you know, like a message in a bottle—and then it pops open again, kind of like those tents kids play with, and it catches the blood—when you're on your period, I mean."

He stared. "I... have never heard of that."

"It's all the rage. Very environmentally friendly. And much more convenient than tampons." All true; all irrelevant to her current situation.

Nik cocked his head to the side. "And you expect me to believe, Aria, that you are so horribly embarrassed about your little cups, you sat on a box to stop me seeing them?"

"Well—"

"Last night you told me about the time you lost a vibrating egg up there and had to lay it like a chicken."

Her cheeks flushed. "I was *drunk*!"

"Barely. What's in the box?"

"Oh, for Christ's sake." She'd had quite enough of his knowing stare and his sexy smirk. Plus, the corners of the sox were *really* digging into her bum, and frankly, he was right—she wasn't embarrassed about anything. Not bloody menstrual cups,

80

not the various items she'd lost in her vagina, and definitely not the toys she used for her perfectly natural activities.

All of which inspired Aria to stand up and snap, "It's my sox. Are you happy?"

Nik stared down at the slightly squashed box on the bed. Or, actually, at the assortment of sex toys inside it. "Your what?"

"My sox. My sex box. Get it?" He didn't reply. He didn't even look at her. He appeared to be mesmerised by the dildos. "Me and Jen made it up," she added, "when we were younger."

"Jen," he said finally. "The friend who got married on the day we met."

"Yes."

He fell back into silence, but she didn't think he was considering Jen and Theo's holy matrimony. In fact, if his mind was behaving anything like hers, he'd be thinking about that kiss. Their first. The one that had carved out a place for itself in the dirtiest corners of her memory, where it radiated a constant, thrumming pulse of heat.

That kiss, Aria decided woefully, was where all of her problems had begun.

Problems? If problems always came with a gorgeous fake boyfriend and enough money to give you your dreams on a platter, the world would be a far better place.

Okay, true.

She ran her tongue nervously over her lip ring as Nik reached out and—*oh, God*—picked up the purple vibrator she'd dropped. He stood, his eyes on the thick dildo in his hand. Then he ran his thumb over the rabbit's ears and asked, "What is this for?"

Aria couldn't decipher his tone, but she managed to sound lighthearted as she replied, "Figure it out."

He looked up, something dangerous glittering in his eyes. "Why don't you explain it to me?"

81

Aria bit down on the insides of her cheeks, barely resisting the urge to press her thighs together. Something about that low, smoky voice was flooding her pussy with need, swelling her already sensitive clit. Surely, he wasn't coming on to her right now, was he? No. He just liked to tease. For all his supposed playboy ways, she had yet to see any evidence that Nik understood seduction. Not when he was on the receiving end of it, at least.

She didn't usually mind his flirting, but right now she was too close to the edge for games. Time to lighten the mood. Aria injected a spark of humour into her voice and nodded at the toy as she said, "Intimidated?"

"No," he replied. Simply. Instantly. He didn't sound cocky, or even confident—just unconcerned, as though he couldn't imagine why he would be.

Considering the glimpse of him she'd gotten last night, Aria wasn't surprised. The memory dragged her traitorous gaze south, just for a moment—which was long enough to notice the unmistakable bulge straining the front of Nik's shorts, the flushed head of his cock visible above the waistband.

Her knees almost buckled.

Maybe he saw, because he reached out and slid an arm around her waist, pulling her close. The side of her body pressed against Nik's chest, his lips grazing her shoulder, his hard cock pushing into her hip. He ran his mouth up the length of her throat, his tongue gliding over her skin.

"Fuck," she breathed, the pulse of desire between her thighs becoming a pounding rhythm.

"Did you sneak up here to play with yourself?" he asked, obviously amused.

"Clearly, I did," she gritted out.

"Were you going to lie in this bed—*our* bed—and make

yourself come, chrysí mou? Without me? I should make you pay for that."

She dragged in a shaking breath. "Why?"

Nik's mouth sucked gently at the base of her throat for a moment, sending little arrows of sensation flying through her veins. Then he released her with a mocking tut, and said, "I don't think you understand how much I—how much I'm willing to do for you, Aria. I certainly won't let you fuck yourself." He put the toy on the bed, then cupped her cheek in his hand and murmured, "I'll do it for you."

Her mind unravelled like a spool of thread dropped to the floor. "You'll... do..."

"If that—" he flicked a glance at the toy "—is what you want, I'll do it for you. Would you like to come?"

"Yes," she breathed, the word spilling out before she could stop it. "Yes, I want to come."

"Next time," he said, "just ask." He pulled down her bikini bottoms without hesitation, his hands rough. When the fabric fell to her feet, he grabbed her arse and pulled her tight against his body. Their kiss was hot and hard enough to make her shake. His tongue thrust against hers in a rhythm that should've felt crude, too suggestive, too dominant. She melted against him like he was licking into her pussy instead of her mouth.

A second later, he spun her around to face the bed. His hands, surprisingly gentle, pushed her until she bent forward, her upper body resting against the mattress, her arse thrust out lewdly. He picked up the toy, and then she couldn't see him anymore—but she could feel him right behind her, and one of his hands roamed over the curve of her belly.

"Do you have anything to say to me?" he asked softly. For a moment, she frowned, confusion breaking through the haze of lust.

But then she realised he was checking up on her. Making

sure this wasn't too far. Asking for the safe word that wasn't *supposed* to be sexual, and yet, here they were.

Aria shook her head, relishing the feel of the cool sheets against her cheek. "No."

"Good." She heard the creak of the floor as he moved, sinking down behind her. She could feel his breath against her thighs. Then his big hands palmed her arse and spread her wide, and she felt his breath against her slick folds instead. He let out a low moan. "You are so fucking wet."

"I know."

"Why?"

She hesitated. "Why?"

"Tell me why."

Exquisite tension coiled tight in her core. "Because... because I want you."

"Thank fucking God for that," he muttered. A second later she felt the cool, blunt tip of the vibrator sliding experimentally through her folds, growing slippery as it eased over her wetness. When it teased her swollen, desperate clit, she gave a ragged cry, and Nik's head fell forward to rest against her thigh. "Ah, fuck, Ri. Do you need it? Right now?"

"Now," she agreed, the word strangled.

His fingers spread her intimate folds wider. She could almost feel his intensity, could imagine that dark, focused stare. And for a moment she didn't want the toy at all; she wanted his hot mouth, his hands, and his thick cock. God, she wanted that cock.

She didn't get it. Instead, he murmured, "How long have you been like this?"

"Long enough," she gritted out. And then felt a delicious stretch as the vibrator eased into her pussy, painfully slow and satisfying. "Oh, God, more—"

"Can you take it?"

With a frustrated growl, Aria thrust her hips back. Sensation arced through her as she took the toy deeper, her need only growing.

"Fuck," he hissed, as if it was his dick inside her. As if he was experiencing this pleasure. "Oh my God. The way you look right now—"

"Shut up and fuck me," she ordered, but it sounded more like she was begging. She *was* begging.

And he knew it, too.

"Whatever you need, sweetheart." His voice was a low murmur, ripe with wry amusement... and heavy promise. He thrust the toy deeper, until her cries became ragged and her hips rocked back in a desperate rhythm. And then she felt the slight pressure of the rabbit's ears against her tender clit. She tensed in anticipation for a second before he switched on the vibrator and sent pleasure shuddering through her.

"Oh, fuck," she gasped, hearing how high and needy she sounded, lacking the ability to care. "Fuck, fuck, fuck." She could cry, with this thick length buried deep inside her and those sweet vibrations massaging her swollen clit. "Nik, I'm gonna come, make me come, I need to—" Her words turned into a keening moan.

Without warning, she felt the hot, wet stripe of his tongue between her cheeks, *just* missing that sensitive hole. Always, he was a fucking tease. What she wanted was his mouth, hot and unrestrained on that forbidden place. "More," she gasped out, straining toward him.

"More?" He sounded, for the first time, slightly hesitant. "You want—fuck, you want more." His words broke off a second before his tongue found her tight hole, flicking sweet and wet over her puckered flesh, sending daggers of desire through her veins. The pleasure was so intense it seemed almost painful.

He licked her again and again, still driving the dildo inside her, nudging that vibrator against her clit—until infinity stretched and paused all at once, until spiralling bliss became screaming release. Too fast, way faster than usual, and way too fucking intense. But that wasn't the part that bothered her.

No. What bothered Aria was the sound of his name on her lips. She cried out to him as if it meant something. As if he wasn't the kind of man who'd fuck her just to fuck her. And when she was done, he kissed her hip and ran a soothing hand over her spine as if he actually gave a shit.

Knowing him, he *did* give a shit. She couldn't doubt that no matter who Nik slept with, he treated them gently.

But she wasn't the kind of woman who could take orgasms and gentleness and emerge without compromising her ridiculous heart. In fact, she'd learned the hard way that orgasms and gentleness were enough to sneak past her defences in a way that endangered lives.

Maybe that was why panic clawed at her throat. Maybe that was why she blurted out, her voice overly loud in the silence, "Banana split."

He didn't ask questions. He left.

Chapter 6

At That Point It's Just a Bloody Orgy

Nik was absolutely shitting himself, and he had been for... oh, the past eight hours or so. Which was about how long it had been since he'd lost his goddamn mind, pushed Aria way too far, and enjoyed it way too much.

When they'd gotten ready to go out that night, she hadn't said a word about earlier. They'd carefully avoided staring at the foot of the bed, but the straightened sheets weren't enough to erase the memory of her bent over and spread open to his gaze. His touch. His tongue.

Fuck. Nik's fingers tightened around the cold glass in his hand. He settled back into his seat at the bar and glowered into the darkness, watching Aria and Laurie dance. He felt like a stalker. The feeling didn't improve when Aria flicked a glance at him through sooty lashes, running her tongue over her lip ring. She was nervous, or thinking, or nervous and thinking. Probably about him and the fact that he was...

What? Too attached? That he wanted her too much? Could she feel it in his hands, earlier, could she hear it in his voice? Or were his words too obvious? Or was it something else entirely?

He had no fucking clue. Typically, what Nik didn't know couldn't bother him. Right now, it was eating him alive.

With a scowl, he threw back the last of his whiskey and got up to take a piss. Kieran was hovering protectively around the girls as usual. Nik wasn't worried about leaving Aria here alone with the Fearsome Defender of Women, Children and Kittens around.

Gritting his teeth against the jarring thud of some blaring dance track, Nik made his way down to the toilets. "I should just ask her," he muttered. "That's what I'll do." He didn't know why he hadn't already. Usually, when he was unsure or confused, he spoke up. When he had a question, he demanded an answer. But for some reason, when he'd come upstairs to get ready and laid eyes on Aria again... the words had just dried up in his throat.

And then she'd flashed him a smile and asked if he thought her hoop earrings were too big, or too small, or some shit like that. And he'd thought, *if this is what you want to do, I'll do it.*

Just a few hours later, he was changing his mind. It wasn't as if he could forget what had happened; that would require a hard blow to the head with a big fucking brick. Aria was the person who made him feel calm, who let him breathe and laugh and joke despite the looming dread that was the rest of his life. Being on edge with her, leaving things unsaid... it felt like leaving an open wound unstitched and letting it bleed out all over the place. He wanted to know what she was thinking. He *needed* to.

Nik was starting to understand all that crap his sister liked to say about sex being a 'spiritual experience', because right now it felt as if his soul was tied to Aria's, and something from her end was tugging hard.

"What'd the pisser ever do to you, old friend?"

Nik didn't even look up at the sound of Varo's voice. He just kept glaring at the urinal in front of him. "Fuck off. Unless you want to suck my dick."

"Right now?" Varo's laugh echoed off the washroom tiles. "I'll pass. I don't think Aria would be happy about that, anyway."

"I don't know if she'd give a fuck, to be honest." He zipped up his jeans, turning towards the sinks and coming face to face with his friend. "Why are you loitering down here?"

"I was just about to leave, actually, when you came storming in like a thunderclap." Varo arched one thick brow. "Girl trouble?"

"Something like that." Nik was able to ignore his friend's answering silence for... oh, maybe three seconds, before it started to grate. "Fine, yes. I've been thinking about—the future, I suppose." The future he wanted Aria to be in, even though he had no idea what was going on in her head right now. His confusion had no effect on the ravenous thing in his chest that growled *Mine* every time it saw her. "I'm not sure what to do, now I can't play."

Varo shrugged. "So? Take your time, figure it out."

"I want to know now. I want to be useful. I need to have a plan, so I can..." *So I can show Aria that I'm not just a privileged waste of space.* He gritted his teeth and glared at his own reflection, refusing to say that out loud. "Women like men with jobs."

Varo burst into laughter. "Seriously? What, you're worried Aria will leave you because you don't have a job? I think you're just looking for reasons to worry."

That was true, actually. And it probably seemed pretty weird to Varo, because he thought Aria was Nik's girlfriend. He had no idea how tenuous the situation really was, and Nik couldn't tell him.

Still, he tried. He met his best friend's gaze and let the other man see his desperation, his hopeless adoration, how unbelievably out of his depth he was right now. "I'm panicking, okay? I need her more than I should, and I don't know how to explain it to her. It's fucking ridiculous—"

"Why is it ridiculous?" Varo asked, his brow furrowed.

"Because—*Because I don't understand how I can feel like this so quickly.* "Because I don't know how relationships work," he finished. "I don't know what the timeline usually is."

Varo shrugged. "You know I asked Georgia to marry me the night we met."

"I also know that she told you to piss off. And that you still aren't married."

"But she is mine," Varo grinned, "and she hasn't left me yet." The humour in his voice softened for a moment. "Maybe the moral there is, tell her how you feel, and she'll tell you what she's ready for. Just because you aren't on the same page, doesn't mean you can't enjoy the book together."

Nik digested those words and waited for the doubting voice in his head to say something doom-and-gloom-y. Something like, *We're not even reading the same damned book.* But the voice didn't come. Maybe because the fire of his determination, smouldering for a while now, was finally burning bright. Its smoke was more than thick enough to suffocate his hesitation.

He was Nikolas Christou, for fuck's sake. So what if he was falling for his fake girlfriend? So what if he didn't even know how to describe his feelings? It was all a bit bloody intense, sure, but he could handle it.

She made him feel like he could handle anything.

"You're plotting," Varo said, eyes narrowed. "Aren't you?"

"Something like that," Nik allowed with a smile. "Let's go upstairs, shall we?"

They went.

When they all arrived home, wasted and bleary eyed, Aria was the one who suggested they stay up and play a drinking game.

She felt Nik's presence beside her, the way she had for the past couple of hours. He'd gone from avoiding her almost completely to being her shadow, radiating an intensity she could *feel* with every breath. But she didn't dare look up, even as everyone else cheered at her suggestion. She didn't want to see the question in his eyes. She didn't want to let on that she was afraid to be alone with him.

Afraid because she might do something even more regrettable than the unspeakable horror they'd shared earlier. Calling it 'the unspeakable horror,' she'd decided, made it seem slightly less sexy. Even though the lust-soaked memory wouldn't leave her alone. Even though a dull ache appeared between her legs every time she looked at him, as if her muscles recalled the pleasure he'd brought them and wanted to ask for more.

She *had* to call it 'the unspeakable horror.' If she called it something accurate, like 'the best sex of my life', the sky might fall.

They all moved into one of the great rooms, piled down with more booze, shitty pizzas, and questionable kebabs, and Aria wondered if she'd accidentally doomed the household to the most hellish joint-hangover of all time. But she hardened her heart—and her gut—as everyone sat in a circle and argued about which game to play.

Then she felt Nik's hand in hers. She knew it was his. If his constant affection hadn't taught her to recognise his touch, the feel of his hands spreading her open certainly fucking had. Aria looked back before she could stop herself. Meeting his eyes was like taking a hit of some new and exciting drug that would almost certainly kill you. His gaze was so tender, yet sensual, like hot chocolate and whiskey: comfort with a bite.

He gave her his usual rakish grin, but his touch was gentle, almost unsure. Probably because, she realised with a jolt, he didn't know how she felt about earlier. He didn't know that she'd stopped things because she wanted him too much, not the opposite. And if Aria knew anything about Nik, it was that he had no fucking idea how to read between the lines. So, there was absolutely no chance he'd read her *mind*.

That thought, combined with slightly too much alcohol, made Aria climb into his lap instead of sitting on the floor. He wrapped his arms around her as if worried she might change her mind and scramble off again. "Are you okay?" he whispered in her ear.

"I am." She kissed his cheek and fidgeted until she found a comfortable position. By the time she finished, his cock was hard against her backside. Oops. That really had *not* been her intention—but the rigid length turned her mind into a mess, reckless desire swelling between her thighs.

And Nik seemed to know it. He pressed his lips to her bare shoulder, his teeth grazing her skin. When he ran his hand over her belly, she was thrown back to the last time he'd done that—as he knelt behind her and drove her to orgasm with her own fucking Rampant Rabbit. Jesus, that was one hell of a power move. She wouldn't even be able to use the thing without thinking of him, now. And it'd cost eighty fucking quid!

She wriggled around some more, rubbing her arse over his stiff dick, just to spite him. When he released a soft, choked groan, petty satisfaction made her smile.

"Never have I ever!" Georgia bellowed suddenly, cutting through the commotion. "That's what we'll play!"

Across the circle, Shenker scowled. "What are we, seventeen?"

"Shut up, miserable. I have spoken." Georgia stood, which didn't put her much higher than everyone who was sitting down. "Okay, I'll start. Never have I ever had a threesome—wait for it," she insisted over the circle's-tired groan. "Never have I ever had a threesome in public. Yeahhh, who's drinking now, fuckers?"

"You, querida," Varo said.

Georgia blinked. "Oh. Oh, yeah!" She tossed back a shot. So did an impressive number of the circle, including Nik. Honestly, Aria felt kind of left out.

But she redeemed herself over the next few questions. Except for the weird ones, like "Never have I ever swum with sharks." She wasn't surprised when Nik drank to that, either. Personally, Aria would rather live to a ripe old age with only a vibrator and a bottle of vodka to thrill her than run around inviting predators to take a bite, but she tried not to judge.

As the game went on, Nik's hands roamed over her body, so slow and casual that no-one seemed to notice he was essentially groping her. He stroked lightly over her breast, then glided down her ribs. A second later, his fingers would breach the hem of her dress to skate over the sensitive skin of her inner thigh. And then he'd be back at her chest, his fingers nudging her tightening nipples, his lips grazing the dip where her neck and shoulder met.

"Do you need something, agapi mou?" he asked her suddenly. Which was when Aria realised that she'd begun rocking against his erection, desperate for pressure on her swollen, sensitive pussy.

"No," she bit out.

"Mmm," he murmured dryly. He might as well have called her a liar. His hand rested on her hip, feeling hotter than it should. "I don't know why you stopped things, earlier, but I think you still want me. Am I wrong?"

She turned her head, met his eyes, and her sarcastic response dropped out of her head. She was caught, as if in a spider's web—but the trap lay in the expression on his face, the gentleness that belied his teasing tone, as if he really *cared* about the answer. He held her gaze, unflinching, as he waited for a response.

Before she could manage one, the next challenge was shouted in Shenker's deep voice. "Never have I ever had a *fivesome*. Public or otherwise."

Nik's expression soured, and he looked past her to glare at the grinning blond. Then, his face still hard, he drank.

Oh, for fuck's sake. How the hell was she supposed to compete with a fivesome? "At that point it's just a bloody orgy," she muttered.

Nik chuckled, and her cheeks heated. She always spoke too loudly when she was drunk. He kissed her neck, replacing her flush of embarrassment with a different source of warmth. "If I'd known one person could make me feel the way you do," he murmured, "I'd have used all that energy to hunt you down." This time, when she met his eyes, all she saw was hunger. Somehow, she didn't doubt him for a second.

In a moment of drunken clarity, Aria asked herself: how the hell did she get here? Not *here,* as in a pro footballer's debauched house party in Marbella—but *here,* in the lap of a man who seemed to want her more than he should. A man whose desire and affection weren't swallowed whole by the bottomless pit in her chest, whose presence surrounded her like a shield.

Then the moment passed, and she was just drunk and horny again.

"Never have I ever been married," hollered the next girl. Aria grimaced and took a shot. Behind her, Nik stiffened—well, the parts of him that weren't his cock, anyway. That thing was already stiff to begin with.

She giggled at the nonsensical thought. Understandably,

since he couldn't read her mind, Nik didn't laugh along. "For real?" He whispered in her ear.

"What?"

"You're married?"

Aria rolled her eyes. "I'm divorced."

"Aren't you twenty-seven?"

"That's more than enough time to get divorced, sweetheart." She'd been divorced at twenty, as a matter of fact, and married at eighteen. It certainly wasn't the worst decision she'd ever made.

Or the best.

"Who was he?" Nik asked, after a pause.

"My husband." She snickered at the joke, but he didn't join in.

Instead, he asked, "Do you still see him?"

With a sigh of exasperation, Aria turned to look at him. "Do you care?"

She regretted her flippancy immediately—because Nik didn't laugh or even smirk, and he certainly didn't snap back. He didn't say a word, but his expression answered, loud and clear: *Yes.*

"Aria!" Georgia called from across the circle. "It's your turn."

Oh, right. She turned to face everyone as her mind, conveniently, blanked. "Um... Never have I ever..." She really should've thought about this earlier, instead of dry-humping the man who was paying her to be here. "Never have I ever played football!"

The room practically exploded. There were cries of astonishment, of outrage, of what appeared to be genuine disgust—interspersed, of course, with gulps as everyone else downed a shot. Literally, *everyone.* Every single person in the room.

Huh. Awkward.

"Come on, Nik," Kieran yelled. He got louder after a few drinks, it seemed. "What the fuck, man? Bring her in!"

"How are you dating a footballer and you've never played football?" demanded a blonde to Aria's left.

"Well, I doubt Posh has played, either," she said defensively.

"Honey," the woman smirked. "You're not exactly—" Then she caught the expression on Aria's face and suddenly discovered the benefits of silently studying the floor.

Behind her, Nik chuckled softly. He traced the thorny roses climbing her bicep and said, "You realise this state of affairs cannot continue?"

Something inside her relaxed at the unmistakable sound of his smile. Despite his probing questions about her ex, he wasn't... upset. Not that she'd care if he *was*, since he had no right to be.

Except she totally fucking would, because she was a complete sap.

"The football thing, you mean? You're not going to make me play, are you?"

"Of course, I'm going to make you play," he laughed. "Good God, chrysí mou. What do you take me for?"

"Stop talking, you two." Georgia interjected. "Nik, it's your turn."

He sighed. "Alright, relax. Never have I ever..." He smiled as he ran his knuckles over Aria's collarbone. "Never have I ever gotten a tattoo."

Most of the room drank at that one. It was the first time Aria had really considered Nik's lack of ink—usually, when she saw him naked, she was more concerned with his body than his unadorned skin. But suddenly the perfection of such a big, bare canvas hit her.

"I think you should drink twice," he said, his finger circling the little octopus above her knee.

She snorted. "Nice try." But she kind of invalidated those words when she did as he'd suggested, taking the shot he'd just poured for himself. "You should get a tattoo." Aria wasn't in the business of telling people what they should and shouldn't do with their bodies—that was the opposite of her attitude, actually —but the words leapt out anyway.

"You think it would look good?"

"No. Well, yes, but that's not why I..." she trailed off, because explaining her reasoning felt kind of awkward. She hadn't said it because he'd look good. She'd said it for the same reason he wanted her to play football.

He seemed to grasp that without her finishing an impossible sentence. His smile widened, becoming almost shark-like, and he said, "So give me a tattoo."

Aria blinked, certain that she was experiencing some kind of alcohol-induced, auditory hallucination. It had been a while since she'd been *that* drunk, but these people went hard. "You can't be serious."

"I'm dead serious. You're a tattoo artist."

She threw up her hands. "We're in Marbella, Nik."

"But you can tattoo anywhere. The way people do when they're learning, right, before they get a gun or whatever—"

"A machine. Call it a machine. And if you're talking about stick-and-pokes, I don't think that's a good idea."

"You can't do it?"

"Well, sure, I can do it—"

"Then it's settled. Tomorrow." He kissed her cheek. "Try not to kill me."

"How the hell would I *kill* you?"

"I'm sure you could find a way." That dragged a laugh out of her. The sound was cut off by a gasp when he moved without warning, pulling them both to their feet. She looked around the circle and realised that, while they'd been talking, the game had devolved into random drinking and copious make out sessions. Huh. "Upstairs?" Nik asked, packing a thousand words into just one.

She nodded.

Then swallowed a scream as he picked her up.

"You have *got* to stop doing this," she huffed as he strode from the room.

"Why?"

"Because..." Well, actually, that was a good question. Why?

"Don't you like it?" he prompted.

"It doesn't matter if I *like* it—"

"I really think it does." He climbed the first set of stairs, jostling her only slightly. The bouncing must have shaken up her brain, because she finally thought of a response.

"You can't carry me up three flights of stairs and halfway across the house," she said with certainty.

"Is that really what you think?"

She sighed. "You're about to destroy your knee just to prove a point, aren't you?"

"My knee is fine, moro mou. But I appreciate the concern."

She swatted his shoulder. "I already told you to cut the sexy shit."

"You'd take my mother tongue from me?" he tutted sadly. "You English. You think you rule the world."

Was she laughing so hard because of the alcohol fizzing through her veins, or was this a different sort of intoxication? Aria decided not to think about it too much.

By the time they reached the final set of stairs, their steady stream of banter had faded, and Nik's expression had become slightly ferocious. "You're quiet," she snickered.

He flashed her a mock glare. "Excuse me, madam. I'm conserving oxygen."

Her giggle sounded distant, as if it was coming from

someone else. She felt oddly lightheaded as she raised a finger to trail along the line of his jaw. "You're all scratchy."

Nik looked down at her with something that might've been alarm. The expression softened into a smile a second later. "You're wasted," he accused, humour dancing through his words.

"You're pretty," she shot back, tapping the slight bump in the bridge of his nose. Wait—that wasn't how arguments were supposed to go, was it? Ah, well. Too late now.

"You're pretty, too." His voice was like the warmth of a campfire on a cold night.

"Well," she hedged, "I don't know if I'd say *pretty*—"

"You're right." He reached their room and nudged the door open with his foot. "The first time I saw you, I thought you were striking."

"Yes," she agreed enthusiastically as he put her on the bed. He sat her up against the pillows, but she flopped sideways. That felt better. "Striking!"

"I have since readjusted my opinion, though." He was leaning over her, fiddling with her... ear? What an odd thing to fiddle with. There were far more useful places he could touch. "I think 'stunning' suits you better."

Oh, he was taking out her hoop earrings. Good idea. Goooood idea. They were very big.

"Or we could go with a classic," he went on, "and say 'beautiful'. You're definitely beautiful." He took out the second hoop and laid them both on the bedside table. His hand went to the zip at the side of her dress, then stopped. "Do you want to take this off?"

"I do," she nodded. Nod, nod, nod. She reached for the zip, tugged, fumbled. "You do it. And keep telling me how great I am."

He laughed and sat down beside her, easing the zip down carefully. "Alright. I like the clothes you wear."

"Because they are *tiny*."

"Because they're outrageous," he corrected. "But you wear them so casually. If anyone else had walked into that club tonight wearing fluffy, green high heels, they'd have looked ridiculous. But you just looked like you." He pulled her up into a sitting position, resting her back against his chest. "Are you feeling okay?"

"I feel great," she said. And she did. Very warm and tingly inside, from all these very nice words. Also, the booze. "I just got so tired all at once."

"Okay, honey. If you're gonna throw up—"

"I *never* throw up," she said grandly.

"But if you feel like you might, tell me." Her zip undone, he began to peel off her dress, easing her arms out of the spaghetti straps. Aria sighed as inch after inch of confining fabric left her body—

Until he stopped with a muffled curse and yanked the bodice back up. "You're naked."

"No..." she said slowly. "I'm wearing this dress. Kind of."

"Underneath the dress," he ground out.

"No. I'm wearing knickers. Never go out without your knickers. They're very important." She paused. "Although I can see why you *might* go out without your knickers—"

"Aria. Are you sure you want me to take this off?"

"*Yes*. It's tight." She grabbed the fabric and pushed it down, wiggling a little when she reached her hips. She might be mistaken, but she thought she heard Nik muttering to himself beneath the bouncing of the bed springs. He was barely touching her anymore; the palm of his hand splayed against her back like a starfish, keeping her upright, but that was it. He must have a very strong hand, Aria decided. And arm. And shoulder.

She pushed the dress off completely and flopped down on top of the sheets with a sigh. "That's better."

Nik grunted. She turned to find him pulling off his T-shirt in that way men did, yanking it over his head with both hands. Then he stood and took off his jeans, too, moving at lightning speed.

"Are you tired?" she asked.

"Yeah," he said, but his voice sounded a little odd. "Yes, agapi mou. I'm tired."

"Okay." Aria rolled onto her stomach—it truly was the best way to sleep—and closed her eyes, ignoring the glow of the lamp that burned through her lids. She should probably take her makeup off. She'd get mascara all over the lovely white pillowcases. But her body felt so deliciously heavy, all easy and languid like it had after he'd made her come.

The feeling wasn't going away, either, like it had before. With Nik, she'd only enjoyed that sweet relief for a second before she'd turned all stiff and cold with fear. And then she'd sent him away, but she couldn't quite remember why...

"We should've had sex earlier," Aria said, her voice slightly slurred, her thoughts blurring.

"What?"

"I mean, more sex. With sweat. And skin. On skin..." Had he turned off the lamp? Everything seemed so much darker, all of a sudden. "Can we do it tomorrow?"

Even as sleep dragged her under, she recognised the feather-light touch of his fingers against her cheek. "Ask me in the morning, Ri."

"You know I won't ask you in the morning," she grumbled.

"Yeah," he sighed. "I know."

Chapter 7

A Funny Story

"Help me," Aria groaned. "I'm dying."

Nik's soft laugh, while sexy as ever, was not welcome. It was irritating, in fact. Doubly irritating because, even with her head pounding and her stomach sloshing around like an ocean, it still sent a tingle along her spine.

"You're not dying, chrysí mou."

"I *know*," she gritted out. "It's *hyperbole*. For dramatic *effect*." She winced. Ouch. A bit too much emphasis, there.

"Shh." His hand settled against her back, a comforting weight that kept her anchored. She'd been lying in bed feeling as if the room was spinning, but that hand made things a little bit steadier. "I got you some water. And aspirin."

It was a lovely sentiment, and she was thirsty as a mother-fucker, but sitting up felt like a very bad idea right now. "In a minute," she mumbled.

"Come here." The hand on her back became an arm around her waist, easing her gently but firmly into a sort of... sideways lounge. Oh, that wasn't so bad. It wasn't sitting up, at least. Aria cushioned her aching head with one hand and risked opening an eye, squinting up toward the sound of Nik's voice.

The room wasn't painfully bright, thank God. He'd pulled the curtains close, so enough sunlight seeped in to illuminate the room, but not enough to make her headache worse. He was sitting beside her at the edge of the bed, freshly showered and despicably attractive. And even though she must have looked pathetic, at best, there was a heat in his gaze that made her head spin.

Which wasn't great, since her head had already been spinning. In the opposite direction.

His expression changed so fast, she wondered if she'd been imagining things. Now, he looked relaxed and slightly amused, as always, the cocky playboy to a T. Still, she didn't think cocky playboys brought their fake girlfriends precious, precious aspirin after a night of too much drinking.

"Here you go." He held out the pills and watched as she swallowed them dry, his brows raised. "That was... impressive, or maybe terrifying. I'm not sure."

She huffed out a laugh, then instantly regretted it as pain shot through her head. "Habit."

"A habit you learned by..."

She took the water he held and downed it before answering. "By taking lots of drugs, sweetheart."

"Oh." His lips twitched with amusement. "You must think I'm very boring."

"Because you never popped questionable pills in filthy bathrooms so your parents would pay attention to you? No, Nik. I don't think you're boring." To be honest, she'd rarely met anyone she found so entertaining. She could be locked in a room with nothing but him and the bloody Yellow Pages for twenty-four hours, and they'd have a cracking good time.

Even if they kept their clothes on.

He took her empty glass of water and produced another like some kind of hydration fairy. "I think we should stay in tonight."

Talia Hibbert

"No. Noooo. You're not missing out on your friends' weird hedonist explosion, not on my account."

He combed through her tangled hair with his fingers as he replied. "I'm in charge, Ri."

"You're a pain in the arse, is what you are."

"Never. I always take it slow." He dropped a kiss on her forehead and the surprise of that unnecessary affection was almost enough to make her miss what he'd said. "I'm going to make breakfast," he told her, standing up.

He'd reached the door before her kiss-addled brain lurched back into action. "You're—you—stop making dirty jokes!" Okay, maybe her brain wasn't *quite* at full capacity just yet, but whatever.

He paused in the doorway. "Do you mean that?"

She wished he hadn't asked. She wished he'd just... assumed. Or ignored her. Because now she had to think about it, and realise that she *didn't*, and explicitly say, "No. No, I don't mean that."

At which point, he gave her a knowing glance over his shoulder. "Thought not."

She threw a pillow at him as he left. The action probably hurt her head more than it hurt his retreating back, but really, it was the thought that counted.

By the time Aria felt human again, the rest of the household was getting ready for the night's events. Nik brought her a bagel covered in chocolate spread—because she still hadn't gotten out of bed yet—and said, "Georgia sends her love."

"That woman is trying to make me fatter," Aria grumbled as she ripped into the bread.

"If you're waiting for me to complain, you'll be disappoint-

104

ed." Nik settled onto the bed beside her and picked up half of the bagel before she could stop him. "Thanks."

"For *what*, you thief? Didn't I warn you about stealing my food?"

"That was before," he grinned, humour glinting in his eyes. "This is now."

"What on earth is the difference between then and now?" As soon as the words left her mouth, she wanted to take them back. There were a hell of a lot of answers he could give to that question.

But all he said was, "You *like* me now."

"I liked you then," she admitted, "for reasons that escape me."

"Yeah?" His head rested on a pillow beside her crossed legs. He bit lightly at her knee, just the barest scrape of teeth, but it still sent a thrill straight to the place between her thighs. The place that suddenly felt more like a *space*, conspicuously empty, needing to be filled.

For God's sake. Was that all it took her get her going, now?

"Things have changed between us since we met," he said, looking up at her. His eyes were like honey in the sunlight streaming through the window, golden-brown and sticky-sweet enough to trap her. "So, if you liked me then, how do you feel now?"

Aria bit her lip. Something was dragging her gaze, like a magnet, toward the place at the foot of the bed where he'd bent her over—but she wouldn't give in to that pull. Because if she did, he'd see, and he'd know exactly what she was thinking.

Instead, she said honestly, "I *really* like you now."

"So, once this is over," he said, "and you go home to start the best tattoo shop in Europe—"

She laughed, and his teasing smile widened.

"In the *world*, actually," he corrected. "Once that happens…

you won't be done with me." It didn't sound like a question, the way he said it. And that cocky grin on his face, that solid confidence in his tone, didn't suggest any kind of uncertainty.

But she must not be fully recovered from last night, because she imagined she saw uncertainty anyway. Imagined she heard it. Imagined she *felt* it. "Are you asking if we're friends? Real friends?"

"Yeah," he said softly.

Aria ran her tongue over her lip ring. "I'd like us to be. I don't want to never see you again." Actually, just the thought made her feel sick. Or maybe that was the chocolate bagel she was currently scarfing down? Must be. Still, the prospect of him disappearing was... unpleasant.

"I feel the same way," he said, looking up at the ceiling. "Do you want to hear a funny story?"

She chuckled nervously at the abrupt change in subject. "Um... okay?"

"A few years back, I met this girl—French girl. I don't speak French. But she was a huge Colston City fan, so she sat on my lap at a party and..." He shrugged. "You know. At this point, I was living with Kieran. So, the next morning, she leaves my room to get a drink. Half an hour passes, and she's nowhere to be found. I get up, go looking for her... and she's still in the kitchen, talking to Kieran. *He* speaks French. Anyway, I knew he was going to be precious about it, so I pulled him aside and told him he should ask her out. He refused, because of some weird friendship code, so I asked her out for him. And—"

"Is this your weird way of telling me you slept with Laurie?" Aria interrupted.

He flashed her a sheepish smile. "Yeah. Yes, it is."

She chewed on the last bite of her bagel, then snatched the other half from his grip. He'd barely eaten it, anyway. "Okay."

Was that relief on his face? Maybe, but it was quickly replaced by grim determination. "Here's another funny story."

"Oh, Christ." Despite herself, Aria felt a grin creep onto her face. "Go on, then."

"So, you know Varo's my best friend, right? And he fell in love with G at first sight. They're a forever kind of thing. But Georgia's into threesomes, and—"

"You *cannot* be serious right now."

He spoke faster, ignoring her spluttering. If she didn't know any better, she'd think he was nervous. "Georgia's into threesomes and Varo is too, but he's protective. Plus, he's not out. In fact, I think he considers himself straight. Which means they can't just fuck *anyone*—"

"So, you, being the best friend on earth, volunteered as tribute?"

"That's it," he said. "That's literally it. That's *all*. I like them, they like me, sometimes we fuck."

Through the haze of her shock and amusement—and, yeah, jealousy—Aria realised that Nik had lost his usual grin. His words sounded kind of... edgy? Urgent. As if it was important that she believe him, that she understand.

She felt something light and airy surround her heart, even as a slow smile spread over her face. "Nik why are you telling me this?"

He blinked up at her as if the answer was obvious. "Well. I thought you'd like to know. Because..."

When that word trailed off, a thousand potential endings to his sentence filled her mind. All things considered, one seemed more likely than others.

"Because you're trying to get in my pants," she said. "For real."

"I already got in your pants. Wait, sorry—is that disrespectful? I'm just saying. I mean, I'm just pointing out the fact that I—"

She peered at him closely as he actually *stammered.* Nik Christou was lying beside her, cheeks flushed, fumbling for words as if he were a normal human being instead of a millionaire pro football player who could cosplay Adonis with nothing but a gold laurel.

Aria set the rest of her bagel aside and put a hand over his mouth.

He stopped talking. Then he flicked out his tongue and traced a line over her palm, eyes dancing with mischief.

"You are absolutely impossible," she told him sternly.

He replied with something she couldn't interpret, since her hand was still covering his mouth.

"I thought you weren't doing the casual sex thing anymore?"

Apparently, he wasn't prepared to answer that with a mumble, because he tugged her hand gently away. Eyes burning into hers, he said, "I don't want casual."

Well, smack her on the backside and call her Marianne. "Um... right... so what you want is...?"

"Un-casual. What's the opposite of casual? I want you intensely. I want you *formally?* I want—"

"Committed," she finished, her voice flat. "The opposite of casual is committed."

He studied her for a moment, his gaze sharp, considering. She waited for his inevitable recoil, or maybe some hysterical laughter. It didn't come.

Instead, he said, "Tell me about your ex-husband."

It was an odd request, but she was prepared to go there if it meant a reprieve from this conversation. A reprieve from the tension of knowing that he couldn't want commitment and she definitely shouldn't.

"His name was Matt. We went to school together. He spent

years calling me fat and ugly. Then we turned sixteen, and I don't know what changed, exactly, but all of a sudden, he was into fat and ugly. And I..." she rolled her eyes. "I was pathetic. Trying really, really hard not to be, but I hadn't quite gotten the hang of that whole 'backbone' thing just yet. I thought being with him would mean... winning? Showing everyone who ever laughed at me? I don't know. We were together for years, and I guess we were in love. He never bullied me again, at least. He treated me okay. We ran off at eighteen to be roadies—he was a musician, you see, and he didn't want to be without me. I just wanted to escape my parents."

No, that wasn't true. Aria forced herself to meet Nik's gaze, ignoring the tempest of emotions in his eyes. The sympathy, the tightly contained anger, and something else she couldn't bring herself to focus on. "Actually, I thought it was romantic that he wanted me around. I had— I kind of have a problem, I think. I need to be wanted. I suppose I didn't get enough attention as a kid." She laughed, even though there was no 'suppose' about it. Aria knew exactly what was wrong with her. Funny how that didn't make it easier to fix. "Anyway, we got married, but it didn't work out. I was never going to be happy at that point in my life, no matter who I was with. He's an okay guy. We don't talk, though. We don't have any reason to."

They'd never had any reason to be together in the first place. He'd been in lust, and she'd been in her toxic brand of 'love'. Ah, sweet romance.

"That doesn't sound pathetic to me," Nik said finally. "It sounds like you were vulnerable. But that's okay. You don't learn how to ride a bike without falling."

She smiled despite herself. "Deep, man."

"So deep," he deadpanned.

"Seriously, though, I'm..." Aria trailed off with a sigh. This wasn't fucking therapy. Nevertheless, something about the look

109

on his face made her finish. "I've learned, over the years, that relationships really aren't for me. I'm not... I can't trust myself."

"Yourself?"

"Or anyone else," she added with a grin. "Whatever. Semantics. This is depressing. Can we move on?"

"We can do whatever you like, moro mou." Nik sat up suddenly, their faces inches apart. "I told you yesterday. All you have to do is ask."

His gaze held her hostage, heavy-lidded and intense. Aria's nipples tightened as she squeezed her thighs together, that familiar ache strengthening instantly. "Really?"

"Really." He brushed a kiss over the corner of her mouth. Just the slightest touch, but she felt that hint of pressure directly between her legs.

"Fuck me, then," she said, throwing the words out like a challenge. He couldn't resist a challenge.

Except, apparently, for right now. Nik's mouth met hers, his tongue tracing a red-hot line over the seam of her lips until they parted for him. He didn't deepen the kiss, though. Christ, at this point, she would've let him shove his dick in there—but instead, he pulled away.

A teasing smile on his face, he murmured, "I will fuck you happily. After I take you to dinner."

Aria stared. "What?"

"Dinner." He got up and headed for the wardrobe. "Get up. We're going to eat."

"I... I thought we weren't going out tonight." *I thought you were going to shag me senseless, you infuriating bastard.*

"Not with them. But you're hungry, aren't you?"

Well, yeah. She usually was. And she certainly wouldn't give him the satisfaction of asking for sex again.

Especially not when something in the tightly coiled muscles

of his shoulders, the dangerous gleam in his eyes, told her she'd get what she wanted eventually.

After dinner, she supposed.

"Fine," Aria allowed, dragging herself out of bed. "I'm gonna shower."

"Leave the door open."

She stopped in her tracks, turning to him with a blink. "Why?"

"I know you want to come, Ri. But you won't be. Not until I say so." He rifled through his shirts in the wardrobe as he spoke, his tone casual. "So, leave the door open. If I catch you misbehaving, there'll be consequences."

His voice flooded her body with desperate lust, need pooling low in her belly. Still, Aria kept her voice steady as she said, "Consequences?"

He looked over his shoulder. "Should I spell it out for you, agapi mou?"

"No," she muttered, hurrying off to the shower. She was already horny enough, thanks very much.

Chapter 8

The Greek Thing

N ik took Aria to the best restaurant he knew and wondered why the food tasted like dust in his mouth.

Probably because it wasn't her. Wasn't her skin, sweet and sharp like cinnamon. Wasn't her mouth, soft and inviting. Wasn't her cunt, whose scent was practically imprinted on his brain despite how many hours had passed since he'd made her come.

He might have avoided those sorts of thoughts—and thus avoided getting hard in a five-star restaurant—if Aria hadn't spent the entire meal moaning over every mouthful she swallowed. She gasped as she licked creamy dessert off her spoon; batted her eyelashes every time she looked at him; said his name almost as breathlessly as she did when she came. She was doing it on purpose. Which just made it hotter.

"So, what are you going to do now?" she asked, trailing her fingertips over the stem of her wineglass. She'd had it filled with water because *"If I drink anymore this week, my kidneys might shank me."*

Nick tore his attention away from the glide of her fingers over glass. "Do?"

"Instead of football," she said slowly, which reminded him that before the movement of her hands had hypnotised him, they'd been discussing his profession.

"Ah. Right. Well, that's the question, isn't it?"

She arched a brow. "You don't have any ideas?"

"No," he said, both entirely honest and slightly pathetic. "I, um... I'm not really good at anything else."

He wasn't expecting those words to produce such an outraged expression from Aria. She looked personally offended. "What on earth are you taking about? Yes, you bloody are!"

Even though she was wrong, his heart swelled, a smile curving his lips. "You think?"

"Oh, come on. You *know* you are." She gave him a suspicious look, as if this were all part of some ploy. Like he was fishing for compliments, or something. But after a moment, she seemed to realise that he was deadly serious.

"I told you before," Nik said. "My life has been easy. Football is my only skill and I was lucky enough to be able to pursue it." He shrugged. "I don't know what I'll do next. I'm working on it. It's just taking me a while because every time I try to think about the future, I freeze. I can't see anything." *Except you. I see you like a light in the dark.*

"Ah." She nodded slowly. "Well, that's totally understandable. Your career just ended abruptly. You've lost your passion. But you're amazing, Nik. There are a thousand things you could do, related to football or otherwise—you're the most determined person I've ever met. You can do anything. *Anything.* So, don't pressure yourself, don't overthink it, just... take some time to acclimatise. Let yourself breathe. Okay?"

He managed to force out some sort of agreement, even though emotion clogged his throat. She hadn't said anything that he didn't know already. But he only knew it *logically*; the words had never sunk into his bones before. To have Aria, the person he trusted most in the world, tell him that it was okay? That he could handle this? That he'd be alright?

A tension Nik hadn't realised he'd been carrying drifted away. He felt suddenly lighter, stronger, more like *himself*, than he had for weeks. She moved the conversation on, the sound of her voice soothing him even though he couldn't discern the words. He was thinking too hard. He was considering a new approach, a new plan, a new way to become the person he wanted to be.

Eventually, his whirring thoughts stilled. He didn't need to work on this now. He had time. Everything would be fine. Aria had said so.

He took a breath that felt as refreshing as cool rain and said, "Thank you."

She didn't ask what for. She didn't point out that they'd been talking about something else entirely for the last five minutes—or rather, that she'd been talking, and he'd been grunting occasionally while staring at the tablecloth.

Instead, she smiled and said, "Any time."

The rest of the night flowed like water.

Was it odd that taking her out, ordering whatever she wanted, showing her places she'd never been before, soothed the hunger in his chest as much as touching her did? Maybe. Nik was starting to think he'd fallen in love with her. Not now; before. Ages ago. He'd always thought that when he fell in love, he'd know—just like his parents had known, just like his sister had known. But he wasn't the smartest guy in the world.

As she teased him throughout dinner, as he drove them home with his hand on her thigh, Nik considered the possibility that he'd fallen in love without noticing.

It did *sound* like something he'd do. The idea bore further investigation.

They parked up and headed into the house in uncharacteristic silence, the razor-edged flirtation they'd kept up throughout the night finally fading. He knew why. For the past couple of hours, a glimmering thread of tension had stretched taut between them, crackling like a live wire. Now someone would have to make the first move. Someone would have to risk a shock.

"No-one's home," she murmured as they wandered through the house.

"It's barely ten. They probably just left."

"We'll be alone for hours." She climbed the stairs ahead of him with a slow, lethal smile.

If Nik's cock could get any harder, it would have. "You want me to fuck you now, agapi mou? Should I push you to your knees on the stairs, pull your underwear aside and shove my dick inside you?"

He heard her sharp intake of breath and wrapped a steadying arm around her as she faltered.

Pressing his lips to her ear, he murmured, "I could. But I won't. Upstairs."

Because he had this weird, old-fashioned idea that the first time he fucked her, it would be on a bed. He'd never cared about that kind of thing before, because it didn't matter—but this woman. This fucking woman.

He reached out and pulled up her skirt. The tight fabric caught around her waist, and he moved down a step to take in the sight of her arse, the dimpled globes bisected by a strip of blue silk. She arched her back and looked over her shoulder at him, challenge sparkling in her eyes. "I dare you."

He spanked her, not particularly hard. "Nice try. Up." He wouldn't be distracted tonight. He knew exactly what he wanted, and he was going to get it.

She laughed—the best fucking laugh he'd ever heard, like a waterfall of freedom with a stormy edge of lust—and then she moved again, climbing the stairs faster than he'd ever seen, that luscious backside bouncing with every step. On the second flight of stairs, she stumbled again with a giggle. He steadied her from a few steps below, reaching up to put his hands on her waist. Then he bit her thigh, just hard enough to make her gasp.

"You really are impossible," she accused, but she didn't sound unhappy about it.

"And you're irresistible. Here we are together. I wonder what will happen next."

"Shut up," she snorted, climbing the stairs again and skipping across the landing.

"You can shut me up when we're in bed," he said mildly. "You can suffocate me with all that, if you want."

"I just might."

The idea sounded like heaven, actually, filthy fucking heaven: Aria sitting on his face. He'd breathe in her cunt like it was oxygen and die with her thighs holding him hostage. Yeah. That was his new life goal. But maybe he'd save it for sixty years' time. There were a lot of things he needed to do before he died, after all.

Like marry Aria Granger.

The thought didn't even faze him. The exact fucking opposite, in fact. A grin slid over his face as he followed her up the last few steps—until he remembered that marrying Aria would be difficult when she didn't even want to be with him.

Or anyone, it seemed. A couple of hours ago, she'd said the word 'commitment' like it was a slug she'd had to pick up with her bare hands. Nick hesitated as they reached the top of the stairs, suddenly worried. And quite disturbingly sure that his earlier suspicions were correct: he *was* in love with Aria.

He was in love with Aria.

Perfect.

On the landing, he reached out and caught her wrist. She

turned back to look at him, those almond eyes wide and questioning, her glossy lips parted. God, those lips.

Nik shook his head, forcing himself to focus on words—actual, useful words. Hopefully some of the blood in his body had remained in his brain, rather than relocating completely to his throbbing cock.

"Listen, Ri, what I said earlier... I meant it. This isn't casual."

"Okay," she said slowly, almost nervously. "So, what is it?"

Love, his ridiculous mind supplied. Like he could say that to her, when she flinched at the thought of a relationship. "It's us. It's just you and me."

The words made not a lick of sense, but something about her seemed soothed, and he saw understanding in her eyes. "Yeah," she said softly. "You and me."

That settled, Nik gave into the need heating his blood and pushed her gently back, back, back, until she was walking through the door of their room. He kicked it shut behind them and dragged her close, hands kneading her luscious arse, cock thrust hard against her belly, tongue tangling with hers. And she met him move for move, just as hungry, just as reckless, pouring her moans into his mouth as if she knew how they fed him.

But she couldn't. She couldn't possibly know what it did to him, to touch her, to be touched by her. If she did, Nik had no doubt, she'd run.

Aria loved sex in general and orgasms in particular. Yet, despite her appreciation for bedroom activities, she wasn't a *Rip off my clothes and fuck up my hair* kind of girl. Mostly because her clothes were too fabulous to mess up for something as common as dick. Also, because she'd never been swept away quite that badly, never been so high on desire that she forgot to care about anything else.

Until now.

When Nik broke their kiss to drag her dress roughly over her head, it didn't irritate her; it pulled a gasp from her lips and sent a thrill racing down her spine. When he threw the dress away and looked down at her near-naked body with hunger in his eyes, she felt her pussy get even wetter. Her underwear must be a mess.

He'd probably like that.

Nik grabbed her hips with both hands, little sparks of electricity zinging from each indent of his fingers in her flesh. "You're so fucking beautiful."

"And you're a tease." Aria leant forward until her tingling nipples brushed his shirt, the cotton rasping against those sensitive tips. When she closed her eyes and moaned, Nik's teeth caught her lower lip. He bit, sucked, and she felt every taut pull as if he'd wrapped his lips around her clit instead.

Releasing her, he slid his palms up her body until they cradled her breasts. "If you want something, agapi mou, just ask."

"I'm not falling for that one again."

He grinned. "Am I not giving you what you wanted?" Before she could reply, he bent his head and gave her nipple a long, wet lick.

She moaned and watched him lap at her breast, his amber skin flushed, his dark brows furrowed and ferocious. Attraction and need coalesced in her core to form something else, something greater, something that had her raking shaking fingers through his hair and panting, "Fuck, yes, please."

He moved to her other breast, one hand pushing up the small, soft mound until it met his lips. His free hand cupped her pussy through her sodden underwear, the fabric clinging to her folds. A flush spread over her chest at the ealization that she was even wetter than she'd thought, that her thighs had grown slick, too. But it was his fault. He'd made her sit through dinner watching those full lips move, remembering the way they felt gliding over her skin. He'd done this.

He knew it, too. Nik sucked her nipple hard and rubbed her pussy, his palm rocking against her clit, his fingers teasing her entrance. Something sensuous and unrestrained rolled through her, stealing her breath.

He released her breast and straightened up, his hand stroking faster now, his lips slightly swollen. "Are you going to come, agapi mou? Already?" He actually had the audacity to use that teasing smile with her right now. He was awful. She adored him.

"Fuck off," Aria managed to gasp, biting back yet another moan. She wouldn't give him the satisfaction. He was already smug enough. But the way he worked her, his touch so satisfying, maybe he had a right to be.

He bent to whisper against her throat, his stubble grazing her sensitive skin. "I love your pretty little tits. I love your fat nipples and the taste of you on my tongue, and I love the way you're riding my hand right now like you might never get the chance again."

She rocked against him harder, the sensation she chased drawing closer with every word. "Ahhhh, Nik, keep—keep—like that—"

"Like this?" he echoed, his tone teasing as ever, but wicked. So wicked. He rubbed her clit in a way that shouldn't have been enough to make her come, only it was, it *was*, because she'd been waiting so long, and she wanted it so much—and because it was him. It was Nik's big hand driving her toward orgasm and Nik's smiling mouth at her throat and Nik's arms holding her upright as she gasped out his name, her knees buckling, her body fizzing away from her like champagne from a freshly-popped cork.

"Fuck, Aria. Eísai tóso ómorfi. You're so beautiful. I need you."

As the last tremors faded and her focus returned, Aria opened her eyes—when had they closed? —and swatted his chest weakly. "I told you about the Greek thing."

He pushed her toward the bed. "You don't want me to be sexy right now?"

"If you get any sexier, I might die."

"Not yet, love. We're not done." He ripped off his clothes as if they were on fire. Aria lay back on the bed and watched, her hand trailing idly down to her still-aching clit, toying with the tight bud through her knickers. First, he stripped away his shirt, revealing that broad chest and the thick trail of hair pointing down his abdomen. His jeans went next, and Aria salivated over his powerful thighs until he finally pushed down his briefs.

At that point, he may as well have been a floating erection. She certainly wasn't looking at any other part of him, not anymore. Because Jesus, she loved his cock. It jutted up against his abs, veering slightly to the left, the swollen head leaking pearly drops of pre-come. Aria circled her clit faster as her arousal spiked again. Impatient, she shoved down her under-wear until she was fully naked.

Nik looked up at her and groaned, his eyes fluttering shut as he tipped his head back. "Oh, fuck." He wrapped a fist around his length, his features drawn tight. "Aria. You don't know what you do to me."

"I think I do," she murmured. And she liked it. So she spread her legs wide and traced her fingertips around her soft, slippery entrance. "Look at me."

He didn't disappoint. Nik's eyes snapped open and he hissed out a breath, biting down on his fist even as he moved closer to the bed. He sank down until his gaze was level with her folds, and when she eased two fingers inside her pussy, he moaned her name.

She released a soft sigh of her own, her hips rocking automatically, her fingers stroking hyper-sensitive walls. "Ohhh, fuck."

"Tell me how it feels," he ordered. "Tell me. Are you tight? Or do you need more?"

"More," she whimpered, thrusting into herself harder. "I want it deeper, but—"

With a growl, he reached out and grabbed her calf, dragging her down the bed. Down, down, down, until her knees were draped over his shoulders and she could feel his panting breaths against her clit. He wrapped a hand around her wrist and pulled her fingers from her pussy, sucking them into his mouth.

Aria moaned as his tongue separated her digits, lapping up every drop of her wetness. She felt his grunt of pleasure as much as she heard it, the deep vibrations setting off tingles of need that scattered through her body. She felt as if she were coming apart at the seams, as if she'd been taken over by pleasure.

"God, you taste so fucking good." He dug his fingers into her thighs, forcing her legs wider. "You have no idea how much I've thought about this."

"Since yesterday?"

"Since the first time I saw you. I spent half the night fucking my own hand." The flash of ferocity in his eyes was raw, almost animalistic. "You're so beautiful, Aria. Tell me you know that."

She was happy with the way she looked—*very* happy, as a matter of fact. She didn't even mind her boobs, as much as she whined about them. But the way he looked at her sometimes, she wondered what he actually saw. Because no-one on earth could be beautiful enough to inspire that kind of urgent desire, to cause the tenderness and the need that battled in his gaze.

"I know," she said softly.

He ran his hands over her thighs, sparking a shiver that made her pussy tighten. Parting her folds, he murmured, "And your cunt. Your cunt's gorgeous too." The crude words set her alight like a match to dry tinder. She was moaning his name even before he finally, *finally* slid his tongue through her folds. But when that hot, wet touch split her open, oh, God, it was good, so fucking good. He lapped at her as if she were dessert and he wanted to savour every mouthful. He licked up the juices spilling from her entrance, his tongue dipping inside her with every few strokes.

And then, when she thought she might die with wanting, when her ragged cries and hoarse demands became truly frantic, he licked her clit. The shock of perfect pleasure as his tongue nudged that aching bud made her scream. *Actually* scream. She'd never even done that before. The sound faded into a desperate, sobbing moan as he closed his lips gently around her clit and sucked.

When he pushed his fingers inside her, she almost came. It was just the barest kiss of that ultimate pleasure, the edge of an orgasm—if that was even possible. Aria had been propped up on her elbows, watching as Nik buried his face in her pussy, but now she fell back with a ragged sigh, her bones turning liquid.

His fingers stroked deeper than hers had managed, but not deep enough to fill the yearning, lustful ache he'd sparked inside her. Still, it was enough to spark tremors in her womb that seemed to shake her bones, tremors that drove every thought but Nik from her head. As she came again, harder than the last time, his tongue moved to lick her growing wetness.

"Fuck, fuck, fuck," she gasped, so sensitive now that she had to pull away. Aria dragged herself up the bed, crawling away from him even as she begged, "Nik, God, Nik, come here."

He kissed her ankle and stood, which was not what she'd

wanted. She wanted him on top of her, weighing her down when she felt ready to float away, giving her more of the pleasure she wasn't sure she could take. Aria watched with frustration as he walked around the bed and produced a box of condoms from the bedside drawer.

"Ri," he said, sitting down beside her, his voice gentler than it had been all night. "I want you to know I'm always safe. With everyone else, I mean."

Oh. She nodded silently, tensing as she waited for the rest. The cajoling *Soooo maybe I could just fuck you bare because look, I really mean it, which means you can trust me enough to throw these in the bin!*

But he didn't say that, or anything like that. He just ripped open a foil packet and put a condom on so fast, she almost missed it. And then, finally, he rolled on top of her, the heat of his body filling a need she hadn't known was there.

He tried to rise up on his elbows, but she wrapped her arms around his neck and dragged him back down. "Like this."

Nik slid one hand into her hair and grasped her thigh with the other, drawing up her leg, opening her to him. The thick head of his cock nudged her entrance, sending currents of electricity through her body. "Aria..."

The expression on his face was almost pained, caught between ecstasy and something else, something too bright to face head-on.

"What is it?" She ran her fingers over his face. Something soft and warm and possessive rolled through her when he nuzzled his cheek into her hand.

"I adore you," he murmured. "Completely. I adore you." His mouth caught hers in a searing kiss as he thrust into her, so fucking slowly. Inch by inch, his cock stretched her wide as his tongue caressed hers. For the first time in forever, she felt full in a way she couldn't describe, a way that had nothing to do with the hard length easing into her.

If he hadn't kissed her when he did, she might have said something dangerous back.

This must be what drowning felt like. Not the part where you choked and panicked and struggled to breathe; this was the part where you gave up, where your mind floated away as your body died, and all you felt was warmth and water and weightlessness. Yes, he decided. Aria felt like a beautiful death and the heaven that followed, all wrapped up in one.

Her kisses were sweet and tender and desperate, her hands sliding through Nik's hair, over his face, his shoulders. Everywhere she touched, she spread star-bright pleasure. He could feel her panting breaths against his cheek, feel her nipples hard against his chest as she arched beneath him. Her hips rocked against his, and his cock—Jesus, his cock was buried so deep in her slick heat, he might never get out again.

That would be perfect; that would be bliss. This, with her, forever.

"Nik," she moaned softly. "Please. Fuck me."

He slid a hand under her head, cradling her skull, holding her to him as he kissed her again. He couldn't speak. If he did, she'd hear the truth in his voice, hear the fact that he loved her in every crack and waver. So, instead, he kissed her, and hoped she wouldn't taste it on his tongue. Holding her tight, Nik eased out of her pussy almost completely, then rocked slowly back into her.

She gave a long, shuddering moan, and he swallowed the sound greedily. The rampant need that had been prowling inside him from the moment they'd met was, for the first time, satisfied. Completely satisfied. He had her. She was his. He wouldn't think about the rest, wouldn't think about reality—*couldn't* right now, with her soft, wet cunt clinging to his dick, and her nails raking his back, and her body trembling every time he thrust.

"Yes," she breathed, breaking the kiss, freeing his reckless mouth. "Yes, oh my God, Nik, like that."

"S'agapó," he breathed. *I love you.*

She sank her teeth into his shoulder for a second, then gave a ragged moan. "I'm going to come."

"S'agapó. S'agapó. Ti mou ékanes, agápi mou?" *What have you done to me, my love?*

He watched her expression dissolve into ecstasy as she came with his name on her lips. Felt her inner walls tighten and release around his cock. He fucked her through it, pushed her higher until she finally relaxed beneath him, completely spent. And then he caught her face in his hands, and kissed her, and gave in to his release.

When he came to his senses, Aria was shoving gently at his shoulder. "Sorry," he mumbled, rolling off of her. To his surprise, she followed, throwing half her body on top of his, burying her face against his chest.

"Goo'night," she sighed, and snuggled deeper as if he were a teddy bear.

"...Ri?"

No response.

"Aria. Are you asleep?"

Apparently so.

Less than five minutes after an orgasm that had shaken his soul, Nik stared up at the ceiling and laughed.

Aria spent the next morning thoroughly enjoying herself. Or rather, thoroughly enjoying Nik as he got acquainted with her sex box.

He seemed to like it. A lot.

By the afternoon, they were up and wandering the streets while the rest of the house slept off last night's excess. As they walked, Nik swung their joined hands with so much enthusiasm, Aria was surprised he hadn't accidentally thrown her halfway across the street. "You're in a good mood," she murmured as they passed cute little stores and cool cafés.

"Of course, I am," he said cheerfully. "I spent my morning coming on your—"

"Will you shut *up*? I don't think those nice old ladies over there need to know about our deviant activities."

Nik barely spared the ladies a look, rolling his eyes. "Deviant activities?" he echoed in mock outrage. "I think you mean love-making, Aria. Very *meaningful* love-making."

She laughed so hard she almost choked. "I'm pretty sure that would involve less dirty talk. And fewer vibrators. And..."

"Don't think I can't fuck the living daylights out of you and make love to you at the same time."

She'd thought he was teasing—he *had* been teasing—only now his voice was low and gravelly, his gaze almost hypnotising. She'd had an unreasonable number of orgasms in the last twenty-four hours, but she felt heat stir in her body anyway, her skin tingling. "Oh."

"Yeah." He pulled her closer, bending down to kiss her nose. "What do you think about that?"

She thought she shouldn't read too much into it, or into the soft look in his eyes. As perfect as Nik was, he was still Nik. Still the biggest playboy she'd ever met—which was saying something —still a man who'd paid her to be here, still the guy who'd practically bent over backward to avoid anything approaching a

What are we? discussion. When she'd mentioned commitment the day before, he'd practically frozen, and then he'd asked about her ex.

Which was fine! Absolutely fine! Because Aria was off men. Off relationships. *Completely.*

"I think," she answered finally, "that you're a man of many talents." She rose up on her toes and kissed his nose right back. Then she let go of his hand and headed up the street. "Do you know how to say, 'India ink' in Spanish, by the way?"

There was a slight pause before he answered, a hesitation before he fell into step at her side and took her hand again. "I know how to say 'India', and I know how to say 'ink'.

"Good enough."

Nik hadn't been joking on that drunken night when he'd asked Aria to give him a tattoo. And he wasn't joking now, either, though she was laughing at what he'd just said as if it were top-tier comedy.

"You want me to *surprise* you?" she repeated, incredulous.

"What, no-one's ever asked you to do that?"

"Well, yeah. The guys who are fucking covered and don't give a shit, sometimes they ask me to do that. But this is your first tattoo, Nik! Don't you know what you want?"

"I think," he said, with complete honesty, "that you'll choose something perfect. Because you're perfect."

Around them, the kitchen erupted into groans. Half the house had dragged themselves out of bed to watch Nik get a stick-and-poke from his girlfriend—and, as always, Nik was using their presence to say things he couldn't usually get away with. He could lavish fake-girlfriend-Aria with praise and have her think it was all part of the act. When they were alone, though, he tried to cool it.

He usually failed, but he tried.

"You know what?" she asked with a wicked smile. "If that's what you want, that's what you're gonna get. A surprise."

"Oh, Christ," Georgia laughed. "You've done it now, Nik. You great ninny!"

Ah, well.

Aria took the whole thing very seriously—but then, he supposed, she *was* a professional. She'd told him all about her apprenticeship, her many tattoos, and how much she loved her job. She was going to open a tattoo shop with the money she'd earned this week. So, obviously, she wouldn't want to accidentally poison him with a needle in a Marbella mansion.

He felt a tickle as she outlined whatever design she'd chosen, but he couldn't see anything. For some reason, she'd decided to tattoo the back of his arm, just above his elbow. He suspected she'd done it to make sure he couldn't see—or maybe so that, if he hated it, it would be easy to ignore. She was the kind of person who thought about things like that.

He wished he could tell her, as she filled the needle with ink and kissed his shoulder, that he'd never hate any mark she put on him.

So why don't you? Why don't you stop fucking around and take what you want? Why don't you tell her that you're not letting go?

Because I want her to hold on, too.

The sharp little pokes began, like scratchy bug bites. He felt her hair brush against the small of his back as she bent her head. He remembered how it had felt grazing his thighs that morning as she rode him, as she tipped her head back and told him she'd never wanted anyone like this.

Soon. He'd tell her soon. Because keeping secrets from Aria was starting to feel like the worst kind of sin.

"Hold still." Aria twisted Nik's arm into the perfect position as she snapped a picture of his fresh tattoo. "I'm gonna post this on Instagram."

"That's great, chrysí mou, but what is it?"

"It's the shit emoji," Varo said solemnly.

The room erupted into laughter. She ignored them and leaned over Nik's shoulder, holding her phone out for him to see. Her heart pounded as she said, "Look."

He peered at the little screen, and she held her breath. She always wanted clients to like their ink, but this was different. She couldn't explain how. It just was. While Nik looked, she studied the image herself, searching nervously for any fuck-ups she'd missed with her naked eye. But all she saw were neat letters inked in fine capitals, spelling out 'Colston City'—the team he'd been so devastated to leave.

She placed her lips by his ear, aware of the whole room watching closely, and murmured, "If you don't like it—"

"I love it."

I love you, she thought, as if it were a natural response. So natural that she opened her mouth and almost let it spill out into the world. Then, thank God, she caught herself and clamped her teeth together. "Great! That's great! Fantastic!"

It was, possibly, the first time Aria had ever held back those three little words. She threw love around all the time, especially in the messy relationships she'd once cobbled together and clung to for reassurance. She'd told *Simon* she loved him, for fuck's sake. The words had never felt heavy on her tongue, had never felt like a spell that, once whispered, could change everything.

They did now. Because Aria had the unnerving suspicion that she might *really* mean it. That she might mean it the way she did when she said it to Jen, or to her annoying little sisters, only different. Different in a way she'd heard of but had never really understood.

Fuck.

She backed away from Nik as his friends surged forward to see the tattoo. She needed to wrap it up. But Nik wasn't an idiot; he wouldn't let anyone touch what was essentially an open wound. She could leave him here for a second while she ran to the bathroom and tried to figure out what the hell was causing these strange feelings in her chest.

No-one noticed Aria leave—except Nik, of course. He always noticed, always found her in a crowd, always watched her from afar. When she scurried out of the door, she felt his gaze on her like a promise. Like the first promise he'd ever made her, one she hadn't believed in at the time: *"I will find you."*

Somehow, in the weeks that had passed, Aria had grown to trust every single word that came out of his mouth. But was that wise? Was it even *real*? Or was she doing the thing she always did, the thing she'd tried so hard to stop after learning just how dangerous it could be?

Aria didn't know. And five minutes staring at herself in the bathroom mirror didn't help matters. No ghostly breath created condensation on the glass; no secret messages appeared. All she saw was her own face, eyes somehow less tired than usual, skin glowing more than it did back home. Must be the vitamin D.

She kind of wished Nik was here, so she could make that horrible joke aloud and he could laugh as if it were funny.

God, this was worse than any crush she'd ever had—if it was even a crush. It felt like she was falling for him. It felt like she was fucking smitten, but that, Aria decided as she unlocked the bathroom door, was a feeling she couldn't trust.

"Aria." Her name, spoken by a voice she barely recognised, was all the warning she had before a big body blocked the doorway, pushing her back.

She was still holding the needle she'd used on Nik, though she'd wrapped it back up in its packaging, ready for disposal. She clutched the little plastic bundle tight as Shenker's pretty face came into view. He gave her an apologetic look as he shut the bathroom door, closing them in together.

"What the fuck?" she demanded.

He held up his hands. "I'm not trying anything. Swear. I just want to talk."

"In a fucking *toilet*? Fuck off before I stab you!"

"Aria calm down. I just need to talk to you without Nik hanging around."

"Why?" she demanded. "What could you possibly have to say to me that my boyfriend can't hear?" *Boyfriend* rolled from her lips far too naturally, but she was too on edge to worry about it.

"I want to warn you," Shenker said.

The words cooled the rage in her blood like a bucket of ice. Warn her? About what? Suspicion unfurled in her chest, its taste bitter and familiar, edged in sour panic. She'd been right to hesitate, to question her feelings. Nik had secrets. He'd been lying to her. He'd been hiding something. She knew it.

"What?" she demanded. To her horror, tears prickled at the corners of her eyes. She blinked them back furiously and speared Shenker with a glare. "Go on. Tell me."

He leant against the door and eyed her with what seemed to be genuine pity. "You know he's just using you, right?"

"How?" she demanded.

"I can tell you're a sweet girl." At her derisive snort, he insisted, "You are! A nice girl. A good girl."

He was saying *girl* rather a lot, considering she was close to thirty.

"Obviously, Nik couldn't use his usual tactics with you," Shenker went on, his tone earnest. "So, he had to try something new. That's all this is, this girlfriend thing. As soon as he gets tired of fucking you—"

"Oh, seriously? That's all you've got?" Aria rolled her eyes, the panic in her veins draining away all at once. Shenker didn't know anything, and he wasn't here to 'warn' her. Clearly, he just wanted to talk crap about Nik, maybe to break up their supposed relationship. Aria didn't know why the two of them hated each other so much, but she *did* know shit-stirring when she heard it.

"I'm serious," the blond said. And he really did sound serious. If it weren't for the fact that, actually, Nik was *paying* Aria to be his girlfriend, she might even believe the guy. "He's never stayed with anyone for more than five minutes. You haven't seen him in action." Shenker's lip curled. "It's fucking disgusting."

"Oh, come on. His sex life offends your delicate sensibilities? Grow up. This whole house is shagging twenty-four seven."

"It's not the same," Shenker spat. "He can't even stay with one woman. Or," he sneered, "one man."

Understanding dawned. Aria ground her teeth so hard, a flash of pain lanced through her skull. "So, what you're saying," she gritted out, "is that my boyfriend's a cheating skank because he's bi. Yeah? Is that right?"

Shenker had the absolute unmitigated gall to *shrug*. As if the question wasn't even worth answering. Which is when her temper really snapped.

Slamming a hand against the door, *right* beside his face, she waved around her little plastic bundle. "Do you know what I have in here?" she asked. "I have a needle. A big fucking needle. And if I put that needle in your eye, it will hurt. A lot. Along with some other unpleasant effects. And you know what, Shenker? I wish I could. I really fucking wish I could stab you right now, more than I've ever wanted to stab anyone in my life. And let me tell you, that's saying something, because I have quite the temper."

He shifted, his jaw set, his expression a woeful attempt to appear unconcerned. She watched his Adam's apple bob as he swallowed.

"Get the fuck out of my way," she whispered, and stepped back.

Without a word, Shenker practically folded himself in half to avoid blocking her path. Aria slammed out of the bathroom and marched down the hall, muttering furiously under her breath.

As she neared the kitchen, Nik appeared, his eyes settling on her with relief. "Hey," he smiled. "Where'd you go?"

She grabbed him by the hand and kept walking, pulling him deeper into the house.

"Okaaaay," he laughed. "We're going somewhere. Cool."

She didn't laugh along. "You said," Aria began quietly, "that you wanted the opposite of casual."

"Uh... yeah," he said, his confusion clear. "I did. I *do*. But you didn't seem big on the commitment thing, so—"

"Neither did you," she pointed out.

"Didn't I?" he asked, his voice a little too mild.

Aria stopped in her tracks, turning to face him. She had no idea what was going on here, not anymore—but she knew one thing with absolute certainty, the kind of certainty she hadn't felt in a very long time.

She trusted Nik. She cared about him. And she would fuck up anyone who messed with him.

Which meant she should probably put on her big girl knickers and say this.

"I want to be with you. For real." Her words were barely a whisper, because although the room they were in seemed empty, anyone might be close by.

But she knew he'd heard her, because his face lit up like a Christmas tree—which was not exactly the reaction she'd expected. She didn't know *what* she'd expected, actually. Something potentially devastating, bad enough that her palms were still sweating even as she saw the happiness in his eyes.

"You do?" he asked, a bit loudly. And then, again, his voice a whisper, "You do? You do. Aria don't fuck with me—"

"Oh, come on. I'm serious. Of course, I'm serious."

He grabbed her, ignoring her shrieked warning about the needle she still held and his brand-new tattoo. "Mine," he murmured against her lips, wrapping an arm around her. "You're mine. You're with me. For real."

"I mean, I thought we could... date," she said awkwardly. "I'll be honest, my relationships are always fucked up. I don't know what we're supposed to do, at this point."

"Well, I've never had a relationship," Nik said, "but I've been thinking about this a lot."

He had? She should probably wonder about that fact, but he was saying lots of lovely things, and their lips were very close. She really had no time for thinking. She was extremely busy.

"You're mine," Nik repeated, "and I'm yours, and we're going to do exactly what we've been doing, and it's going to be great. Okay?"

"Okay."

"Do you trust me?"

She only hesitated for a heartbeat. That barely meant anything, all things considered. "Yes."

Maybe he'd felt that slight pause. Maybe he hadn't. Regardless, when he kissed her, she didn't sense a single reservation from him.

Not one.

Chapter 9

Fraternising With the Enemy

Nik had never been high before, but he was absolutely certain that this was what it felt like. He wasn't dreading the end of the week anymore, counting precious seconds until the moment when Aria walked away from him. By the penultimate day of the party, he'd convinced himself that Aria *couldn't* walk away from him. She was the one, after all, who'd said that they should be together. She was the one who dragged him into unoccupied rooms to fool around all the time; she was the one who curled up in his arms before falling asleep; she was the one who listened to his tentative ideas about the next step in his career and didn't shoot any of them down.

Funny how the transition from a fake relationship to a very real one had gone so smoothly. He almost felt like they'd never been faking in the first place—which, technically, they hadn't. Or rather, *he* hadn't. Really, this was all just a very long and expensive first date, a funny story they could tell their grandchildren one day. At least, that's how Nik was choosing to think of it. He really hoped Aria would see it that way too, because he'd decided to come clean about everything tonight.

He supposed some people might argue that he had nothing

to come clean about. After all, he hadn't lied about himself or his circumstances. He *was* bad at turning people down. He *didn't* want to sleep with anyone else. And she *did* have to scare off overzealous fans for him.

So maybe he could keep his slight dishonesty to himself— except he didn't want to do that. He didn't want to bite his tongue or remember his own bullshit. He didn't want to hide the fact that he'd wanted her from the moment he saw her. And, most of all, he didn't want to abuse Aria's trust.

It seemed pretty fragile. And it was definitely precious.

Of course, he was having a tough time figuring out how to tell her. In fact, pondering that question that made him so distracted, his team actually lost an impromptu five-a-side game on the afternoon before their last day.

"What's up with you?" Kieran demanded with a breathless laugh as they jogged over the grass. "You let Varo past you about a thousand times!"

"Sorry." Nik scowled. "I did, didn't I? I'm just... thinking about stuff."

Kieran rolled his eyes. "You think too much these days. It's not like you."

True. But he was trying to be more thoughtful because certain people in his life deserved it. Nik's gaze drifted over to the seats arranged at the edge of the grass, where Aria sat by a group who were all huddled over a single phone. Whatever they were doing, it apparently didn't interest her.

She was watching him.

And she had that sketchbook in her hands, as always, the one full of all her tattoo ideas. Sometimes, at the end of the day, she'd show him everything she'd done and start talking a mile a minute about her plans for the future, her vision for the shop, how she didn't even know what to call it...

"Hey," he shouted over. "You checking me out?"

She gave him a smirk and shouted back, "I'm wondering how the hell you ever made it if you play like that."

Cheers and hoots of laughter followed her words. Nik couldn't help but grin, even though he usually hated losing. If anyone else had needled him, he'd have been pissed. But right now, he was more enthusiastic about playing than he'd been for the last hour, just because he wanted to wipe that cocky look off her face.

"You don't know anything about football," he reminded her, walking across the grass. "You can't judge me."

"Sure, I can. I'm smart. I pick things up fast."

Nik reached her chair and planted a hand on each arm, locking her into place. As he leaned close, her lashes fluttered and the humour in her eyes became a challenge. He felt an answering tingle in his core, his muscles tightening at their proximity. The possessive beast inside him woke up and pointed out that now would be a great time to drag her into the nearest empty room with a lock.

But he'd already fucked her three times in the past eight hours, and he was trying not to be a complete pest. So, instead of throwing her over his shoulder, Nik darted forward to steal a quick, sweet kiss before straightening up. "Come and play, then. If you're such an expert."

Her eyes widened, amusement replaced by alarm. "Oh, no, I—"

"Go on, Aria!" G beamed. "It'll be fun! We should all play!" She gave a little gasp and slapped her hands to her cheeks. "Girls versus boys!"

"What?" Aria squeaked. "No. Nooo. I've never even played before! And the guys are all pros!"

"So am I," Georgia said.

Aria blinked, her face taking on that adorably baffled look he loved so much. "What?"

"Didn't you know? Most of us are. And everyone knows women's football is way better than men's." She stood with a wink, stretching her arms above her head, and hollered, "Five-a-side, guys! Lads v. lasses."

Nik stepped back and watched with a shit-eating grin as Georgia grabbed a protesting Aria and dragged her towards the pitch.

The afternoon had just gotten a hell of a lot more interesting.

Clearly, Aria's life had gone horribly wrong somewhere along the line. Because if all was running smoothly, she definitely wouldn't be sweating her tits off in a Spanish garden, trying—and failing—to keep up with a bunch of professional football players.

She was going to murder Nik. Brutally.

He'd barely paid attention throughout his last game, but now that she was on the pitch he'd come over all David Beckham. Did David Beckham still play football? She wasn't entirely sure. In fact, due to a tragic lack of oxygen, Aria wasn't entirely sure about anything. Her brain had shrivelled up like a walnut in an effort to keep all of her muscles going.

"Come on, chrysí mou!" Nik jogged by and smacked her on the arse. "Keep moving!"

"Fuck off!" she managed. The words were more mangled gasps than bitten out insults, but she followed them up with a glare.

Nik slowed his pace, jogging backwards as he grinned at her. "You're doing great. You're a natural. You just have to go for it. Stop holding back."

Stop holding back? What, did he want her to throw herself around like he was? "I am *wearing* a *bikini!*"

His gaze darkened as he swept a slow, hungry look over her body. "Yeah. I noticed."

"Aria! Stop fraternising with the enemy!" Georgia snapped as she sprinted past, dribbling the ball as if it were glued to her feet. "Get in the box!"

Ugh. Rolling her eyes and girding her loins, Aria ran.

"You're an absolute bastard."

"I know, sweetheart."

Aria scowled up at the ceiling as Nik sat beside her, his strong hands undoing the ties of her bikini. "Stop fucking humouring me. I mean it! You're a bastard and I hate you."

He released the last tie on her bikini bottoms and slid the fabric out from under her body, leaving her completely naked. "You already said that."

"And I'm going to keep saying it until my muscles stop feeling like pulverised bloody meat!"

"Do what you must, agapi mou." He was trying not to smile, but she could hear the barely contained amusement in his rich, low voice. A second later, she *felt* it, his curved lips gliding over her lower belly.

"Will you behave yourself? I'm absolutely dripping with sweat."

He replaced his lips with his tongue, swiping it over the tan line just above her mound. "Clearly, I don't mind."

She snorted and propped herself up on her elbows, glaring at the top of his head. "I can't believe you made me play and didn't even let me win."

"How could I let you win," he murmured, his lips moving down to her pussy, "when it's a team sport?"

"You're supposed to find a way! You—ahhhh, fuck, Nik." Her indignation was cut off as if a switch had been flicked. Which, if her clit counted as a switch, it had. Nik's tongue parted her folds and found that tight little bud with unnerving accuracy, swirling a hot, wet circle around it. Aria's breath caught as arousal burst to life inside her, forcing her tired legs to fall open.

At which point, Nik stopped licking her and sat up.

"What the fuck are you doing?" she demanded.

He laughed. "I thought you wanted a shower?"

"I *did* want a shower! Until you started stripping me—"

"I stripped you for the shower." He gave her a wide-eyed, innocent look. "I'm just trying to make up for the match. I know you hate losing." God, he was adorable, with that sweet, wicked mouth and those huge dark eyes. The prick.

"*I* hate losing? You're the sore loser in this relationship, sugar." Aria rolled her eyes and clambered off the bed. "Fine. In the shower I go, to masturbate all alone."

"Woah, hold on a second." Nik managed to sound alarmed, mildly offended, and turned on, all at once. "I didn't say anything about *alone*."

She shot him an arch look over her shoulder. "So? Maybe I want to be alone."

"Aria," he growled. God, he was too easy. Just as her feet left the bedroom carpet and landed on the bathroom's cool tiles, his arm snaked its way around her waist. She looked up and found their reflection in the room's huge mirror, Nik's body bracketing hers, his gaze devouring her nakedness. "You don't want to be alone."

She arched back against his hardening cock, biting down on a smile. "I do. You can watch, though. If you want."

Surprise made him falter, just for a second—which was long enough for Aria to pull free of his arms and head toward the shower. She stepped in and switched on the spray as Nik pushed down his shorts on the other side of the glass, freeing his erection. "You're too kind," he said dryly, but the sarcasm didn't quite work when his breath hitched at the end. He gripped his cock so hard his knuckles paled.

Aria turned away to hide her satisfied smile. Nik would bitch and moan, but he wouldn't follow her into the shower, not even playfully. When it came to her body, her emotions—*her*—he did exactly what she wanted and nothing more.

It hit her, like a football to the face, that she felt completely safe with him.

And you love him.

Ah. Now *that* she wasn't sure about. Because it was awfully fast, wasn't it? And she'd had fast before, but never like this.

Although, she supposed, she'd never had someone like Nik, either.

She'd think about it later. It was too difficult to focus on emotions right now, with lust pumping through her veins and him stroking himself on the other side of the glass. Aria reached for the soap, her smile widening into a grin as she saw what stood beside it: one of her many toys, a clear, pink dildo with a suction cup bottom. They'd had a lot of fun with it this morning.

Clearly, its time in the sun wasn't over yet.

"Look what I found." She waved the silicone cock before sticking it to the wall.

Nik released a ragged breath and squeezed his eyes shut, his brows drawing together. "Aria..."

"Open your eyes, love. I thought you wanted to watch?"

When he looked at her again, the need in his gaze was almost enough to make her cave. Especially when he combined it with words, those filthy fucking words she loved so much, tumbling desperately from his mouth. "Let me in. Let me touch you, eali mou. You don't want that. You want me." He jerked his hips up, thrusting into his own fist as if he couldn't control his movements.

Coils of need slid over her body, tightening like rope, making her limbs feel heavy. Aria's pulse pounded in her ears, its rhythm earthy and lustful. Her pussy was so wet, so hot, so swollen, she felt as if she had something wedged between her thighs—as if the cock she wanted so badly had already driven its way home.

But it hadn't. Not yet.

"You've won quite enough today," she told him over the water's gentle spray. "You're getting even cockier than usual. If you want something from me, sweetheart, you'll have to beg."

His eyes flared at the challenge, his hand stroking faster. He leaned back against the bathroom counter and watched her from beneath heavy lids, his mouth easing into a lazy smirk. "We'll see."

Yes, they fucking would. Rolling her eyes, Aria poured out a handful of body wash and let soft, creamy bubbles form. Then she ran her foamy hands over her arms, her movements slow and sensuous and deliberately teasing. It was pretty fucking gratifying to start with something as small as her wrist and have Nik hiss under his breath like she'd just swallowed his cock.

When she started stroking her hips and abdomen, Nik straightened, abandoning his casual posture. He came to stand right by the glass, one hand flat against the shower door as if he wanted to break through. But he wouldn't.

She had a glorious close-up, now, of his big hand rubbing that dark, veined cock. Of the pearly beads of pre-come dripping steadily from its head, making the taut skin gleam. Of his face, lips parted, eyes heavy-lidded and glittering with need.

"Fuck, yes," he groaned when she pinched her nipples with soapy fingers. "Play with yourself for me."

"Not for you," she corrected primly, running a hand over her the curve of her belly. He liked her belly, soft and fleshy and stretch-marked as it was. Just like he liked her tits, tiny and sort of saggy as they were. In fact, Aria realised, he seemed to have a thing for every single part of her. She skimmed her hands over her thighs, and he grunted a curse; she spun around and soaped up her arse, and he banged a fist against the door.

"You want me to come in now," he said, desperation lurking beneath his confident tone.

"No, thank you."

"You do. Bend over, moro mou, let me see your cunt. Spread your legs and—God, yes. Fuck. Don't you want me inside you? I know you do. I know you do."

"No," she lied, standing up and letting the shower wash away all of her soap.

"Look at me, Aria." His voice was smooth as caramel, rich as chocolate, smoky as sin. She turned despite herself and did as he asked. She looked.

She looked at the way his biceps shifted as he worked his own cock. She looked at the desire on his face when he ran a thumb over the slick, swollen head. She looked at his broad chest and remembered the spine-tingling sensation of its soft hair rubbing against her tender breasts.

"Let me in," he murmured.

She shook her head and reached behind her, finding the toy she'd stuck to the wall. "Beg."

"Let me *in*," he gritted out.

Aria bent forward and pushed herself back onto the dildo. Her pussy was so slick that the thick head breached her entrance without issue, just a smooth, slick glide that made her moan low.

Nik's ragged moan joined hers as he watched. "Aria—"

"Beg," she repeated.

His head fell back as he released a strangled growl. And then, finally, he met her eyes and said, "Please. Please, Aria, let me in so I can fuck you until you scream—"

"Why?"

"Because I need you!" he burst out, lust and desperation tangled in his voice.

I need you, too. I want to tell you all the ways I need you, but I'm not brave enough yet.

Soon, though. Soon. Because I know that you won't hurt me when I do. Because I know that I can't hurt myself on you.

"Fine," she said aloud. "Come—"

He didn't even let her finish the sentence.

Nik shoved the shower door open, stepped inside, and slammed it so hard behind him he was surprised it didn't shatter. If it had, he probably wouldn't have noticed. His heart pounded out demands against his rib cage: *need her want her take her have her taste her—*

Aria didn't stand up, didn't ease the toy out of her pussy and come to him, because she was a witch whose purpose in life was to melt his fucking brain. That was really the only explanation. She watched him with a wicked smile on her face as she rode that pink dildo like she was on a mission. A mission to undo him completely. Judging by the drugging swirl of pleasure that had taken over Nik's body, she was succeeding.

She reached out and grabbed his hips, yanking him forward. When her tongue flicked the head of his cock, he buried his hands in her hair and swore. "You want me in your mouth, moro mou? Like this?"

"Yes," she panted, still thrusting against the dildo, arching her back with every stroke.

"Oh, fuck. *Fuck.* You look so good."

She laughed darkly, then wrapped her lips around him and sucked hard enough to make his knees weak. Nik almost bit off his own tongue with the effort it took to keep still, to stop himself from thrusting into the heat of her mouth.

As if she knew what he wanted—*of course* she knew what he wanted—Aria sucked him deeper, the pressure of her lips sheer ecstasy. Nik drew in gasping breaths as she took him inch by inch, her tongue laving the sensitive underside of his shaft. It was strange, to be like this, to *feel* like this—near frantic with lust, mindless with need—and love her at the same time. He'd never had this before, want and adoration intertwined. Not until her.

He liked it. He loved it. He never wanted to lose it.

He couldn't lose her.

Nik swallowed hard as he felt the tip of Aria's nose touch his abs. Her throat worked around him, hot and impossibly erotic, and he waited for her to pull back and gasp... but she didn't. Holy shit, she didn't. She just moved slowly back and forth, sucking him deep and hard, until Nik thought he might die. He might actually fucking die.

And then he ealized that she was touching herself. She was fucking that dildo and sucking his dick and rubbing her clit in tight circles like it was the hottest thing she'd ever done in her life—and Jesus, he couldn't fucking cope with this. "I'm going to come, I'm going to come in your mouth. You want me to?"

He broke off as she moaned, her body arching and stiffening all at once, the hand between her legs slowing, then stilling completely. She was coming, and sucking him harder, and gripping his hip with her free hand as if she wanted to trap him there.

When Nik came a second later, his vision went black.

"So," Aria said, her fingers gliding through his chest hair. "That was fun."

If Nik had had the strength, he would've sat up; it seemed the only way to stare at her with the appropriate amount of astonishment. At the minute, though, he could barely lift his head from the pillow. In fact, he was surprised he'd managed to stagger into bed at all. "*Fun?*"

"You didn't like it?" she asked, apparently innocent. But he knew if he looked down, she'd have one of those sly little smiles on her face.

"Woman. My bones are now 80% fluid."

"Oh dear. That doesn't sound healthy."

"I don't think I'll ever be able to come again."

"How sad for you."

"It's okay," he told her. "The memory of that orgasm will see me through the rest of my life."

"Good to know!" She rose up on her elbows and grinned at him, swooping down to kiss his nose. Then her smile faded into something softer. Her hair, still damp—like the rest of their bodies—spilled over his chest. She brushed her lips against his, all pillow-soft skin and that little ring of silver.

Nik reached up to stroke her face, his heart swelling as he looked at her.

"What?" she asked softly.

"I love you," he replied. Because it was true. Because she must be able to see it anyway. Because it shone from him brighter than a thousand suns, spilling out like champagne.

Aria's brows flew up, her eyes widening, her mouth hanging open. But that was okay: surprise was only to be expected. As long as she didn't jump out of the window or anything, they'd be fine.

Nik threaded a hand through her hair and pulled her closer. "It's okay. You don't need to freak out."

She blinked rapidly before laughing, "Don't I?"

"No."

"Do you always say that after blowjobs?"

He rolled his eyes. "No. I loved you before the blowjob."

"Well, that's nice," she said slowly. "Do you... um..." She actually looked nervous, but he couldn't understand why she would be. "Do you think it's possible, then, to love someone after a week? Well, six days."

"Of course." He sat up slightly, wrapping an arm around her waist. "I've seen it happen before. Plus, my father fell in love with my mother at first sight. And for me... well, I don't think it has been six days. I think I fell in love with you the night we met."

Aria sucked in her cheeks, narrowing her eyes suspiciously. "No, you didn't."

"Yes, I did."

"No, you didn't."

"Yes, I did." He drew out the last word with a grin, and she smiled back. This was going way better than he'd expected.

Aria rolled her eyes, but she couldn't hide her pleasure. She was happy. She was *happy* that he loved her. "This isn't a competition, you know."

"But if it was," he said solemnly, "I would be winning. Because I'm right. And because I fell in love first."

"First?" She arched a brow. "Who says I'm going to fall in love at all?"

His smile didn't falter as he ran a finger over her shoulder, tracing the fine, swirling lines of ink. "Of course you are. I'm handsome and funny and charming—ow!" He scowled as she flicked his forehead, hard. "Do you mind? I'm trying to list my many excellent qualities, here."

"Don't bother," she said dryly. "I'm well aware of all your qualities."

"My *excellent* qualities."

"Sure, babe." But she was laughing now, the sound easing away the tension he'd been carrying. She seemed quite content to stay here, wet and naked and in bed with him.

Perfect.

"Well," she said finally. "I suppose you can love me, if you like. As long as you don't need me to..." She trailed off, frowning suddenly, her tongue fiddling with her lip ring. "I mean, at the start of this week, I didn't even want a relationship. But I—I *like* you more than I've ever liked anyone. I mean, seriously, you have no idea. I wasn't even this into my husband."

He tried not to grin and pump the air. It seemed inappropriate. And slightly juvenile. And definitely not an accurate representation of the joy bursting in his chest; to display that properly, he'd have to set off some fireworks.

"But," Aria went on, "I need to go slow. For myself. I know you do everything instantly, and you're always so sure—"

"Hey," he cut in gently, bringing a hand to her cheek. "It's okay. I didn't say it to pressure you. I said it because it's how I feel, and I want to be honest with you. I always want to be honest with you, agapi mou."

She huffed out a laugh. "I really need to start learning Greek."

"I'll teach you." He kissed her, his tongue gliding against hers before they pulled away. "'Agapi mou'," he murmured, "means 'my love'."

She smiled. "How do you say, 'my hot piece of—'"

Nik covered her lips with his again—only it was more of an awkwardly perfect laughing-into-each-other's-mouths moment.

Then she climbed on top of him and deepened the kiss with a blunt certainty that set him alight. This fucking woman.

"Wait," he panted, pulling away.

Why was he pulling away? He wasn't sure. His cock, especially, wanted an answer, because it had been ready to try for another round already. What a soldier.

Oh, yeah; that was it. They couldn't have sex yet, because he wasn't finished.

"I need to tell you something else," he said. "Actually, it's kind of a confession."

A slight frown furrowed her brow. "What?"

"Well... like I said, I think I fell in love with you the night we met."

She nodded slowly. Was he imagining things, or did she seem slightly tense in his arms, suddenly? He wasn't sure. He was probably just nervous, so he'd better spit this out.

"I knew I was having strong feelings, but I was hesitant, I suppose, to label it? I just knew I wanted you. I really wanted you. In bed, yes, but... like this. Like it is now. So, the next morning I went to find you, but you didn't seem open to dating."

"Okay..."

"And then you brought up the—you know, the human shield thing. That whole, ah, concept." Nik's heart, for some reason, was pounding. And not in a good way. He wasn't used to being nervous about anything other than football. Fuck, after all these years, he didn't even get that anxious before a match; because he was confident, because he trusted himself, because he took things as they came.

But he wasn't confident about this, and he couldn't just take whatever outcome the universe threw at him. There was only one ending to this conversation that he could cope with: Aria deciding that, even though he was a complete prat, she didn't really mind. Or, at least, didn't mind enough to, say...

Leave him. Forever.

Christ, why had that possibility only just occurred to him? Now, when he was teetering on the precipice of confession?

"Well, I saw an opportunity," he said, "so I took it."

She stared. And stared some more. And Nik became uncomfortably aware that he should say a hell of a lot more than that—that he should explain fully, explicitly, and that he should apologise. Except he wasn't even sure if he was sorry.

Yes, I lied to you and brought you here on false pretences, but since you'll be able to start your tattoo shop now, and since the whole plan worked and we're together, and since I love you to fucking distraction, I really don't regret it. I feel bad about it, but I don't regret it.

Did that count as an apology? Nik wasn't sure. He couldn't remember the last time he'd had to make one.

Finally, Aria spoke. But the words were narrow, almost shrunken, her lips barely moving.

"Are you saying that... that you didn't need..." She stopped, sucked in a breath as if steadying herself. And Nik's heart, which had been warm and soft and melting like ice cream, began to cool into something cold and tough.

Finally, she said, "You didn't need a fake girlfriend." She spat out those last two words as if they were a curse, closing her eyes and shaking her head. "Of course, you didn't. Of *course*, you didn't. *Stupid*, Aria, fucking stupid—"

"Love—"

"Don't touch me," she snapped, her eyes flying open to reveal a look he'd never seen before. Not from her, anyway. Never from her. She scrambled out of his lap and off the bed, her face hard. "You made it up. You made it all up just to get me out here and... what, seduce me?"

"Well," he allowed, "when you put it like that, it sounds pretty—"

151

"Dangerous," she said, the word passing her lips like a ghost. "It sounds dangerous. You're..."

Nik felt every ounce of blood drain from his body. His mind searched frantically for ways to control the situation, to fix that haunted, fearful look on her face, to make her see that it was okay. "This was never *dangerous*, Aria. Everything you thought was happening here, that was real, I just didn't get the idea until—"

"Until you needed a way to trap me," she finished, striding over to the wardrobe. He could see, in its reflection, that her look of horror was gone. It had been replaced by a grim determination that sent a chill of fear down his spine.

"Aria. I didn't *trap* you."

"You lured me over here with all your fucking money, so you could have a chance at screwing me," she clipped out, "because you knew that if you asked, I'd say no."

"You still could've said no," he burst out, rising to his feet. His words tumbled over each other, rapid as the beat of his heart. "I just wanted to be around you. But this happened between us because we're good together—"

"This happened between us," she said, shoving on a T-shirt, "because you wanted it to. Because you orchestrated it when you paid me to fawn all over you for a week and sleep next to you—God, I'm pathetic," she ground out.

Nik threw up his hands. "How are *you* pathetic? Don't say that!"

"Don't tell me what to fucking say! I'm pathetic because I'm so bloody *desperate* for affection that I confused fake feelings with actual emotions. I'm pathetic because this whole ridiculous plan worked, and you brainwashed me into wanting you!"

"Aria." The word fell from his lips like a dry, dead autumn leaf. A jagged look of pain crossed her face, and he stepped forward, needing to comfort her.

But she held up a hand and said, *"Don't.* You stay right the fuck over there." She yanked a skirt up her thighs. "Jesus, what is wrong with me? Do I just scream 'easy mark'?"

He'd never felt so helpless in his life. "What the hell are you talking about? I love you!"

"I've loved a lot of people myself," she said. "But I didn't care about them very much."

"What does that *mean?*"

She gave him a sad smile. "It means I want to go home. Now. Without you."

Chapter 10

A Mind of Hearts and Flowers

A ria's best friend opened her fancy front door and beamed. "You're home!"

"Hey, Jen." Aria tried for a smile. She could tell, even without looking, that it was more of a pained grimace. Maybe because she'd cried so much on the journey home—first in the car with Georgia, then alone on the plane, then awkwardly not-quite-alone in the taxi. Perhaps her face was stuck in a frown now.

Or maybe it was just hard to fake happiness when it felt like your chest was cracking open. She should've gotten that hole looked at, back when she was in therapy. Before Nik came along, and saw it, and used it, and broke her in two.

"Wait," Jen said as Aria stepped into the house. "I thought you were due back tomorrow?"

"I was." Aria dumped her luggage. She hadn't been home yet. She couldn't go home yet. "Jenny. I... I'm sorry."

"For what?" Jen stepped forward, frowning, and pulled Aria into a hug. "What's happened? Why do you look so..."

The awkward way Jen trailed off almost made Aria laugh.

In fact, she managed a bitter puff of air that might have been a chuckle. "So terrible?"

"Oh, no," Jen said firmly. "You don't look *terrible*. You've got a cracking tan."

This time, Aria did laugh. Even though it hurt her head and her heart. Even though it felt unnatural, as if she'd never done it before. Even though tears were streaming down her cheeks again. That, Aria supposed, was the power a best friend held.

She buried her face in Jen's soft cloud of hair and admitted, "I lied."

"Oh," Jen said, her voice suspiciously high. "You did?"

"Yes. I didn't go on holiday with some weird new boyfriend you've never heard of." Aria pulled back and met her friend's gaze as she confessed. "I went on holiday with a professional footballer who hired me to be his fake girlfriend."

"Goodness me. Um... let's go and sit down, shall we?" Before Aria could process that suspiciously calm response, Jen grabbed her hand and tugged her through the house.

"Aria's home!" Jen trilled to her husband, Theo—who was sitting in front of a perfectly good TV, reading the paper. The finance section, of all things. Aria really did wonder about that man.

"Hello," he murmured absently. "How was your trip?"

"Terrible," Aria replied, plopping down onto a nearby sofa. "I was just telling Jen how I lied to everyone about my new boyfriend. He was actually one of Keynes's bonkers rich friends and he hired me to protect him from sex at a Spanish house party."

"Wow," Theo said. And turned a page.

Aria glared at Jen, jabbing a finger through the air. "I knew it. You *knew!*"

"No! Nooo, noo, no. Okay, yes. Sorry." Jen scowled at Theo

—or rather, at his paper. "I wasn't going to say anything. It's all supposed to be a secret, isn't it?"

"But..." Aria rubbed her temples. This was, quite frankly, one surprise too many. She was on the edge. She was *past* the edge. She'd flown past the edge less than ten hours ago, when a man she'd trusted, a man she'd—

That's enough of that. Pull yourself together.

Swallowing down her bile, Aria asked, "Who told you?"

"Theo," Jen said promptly.

"And how the hell did you know?" Aria demanded, glaring at the newspaper in front of Theo's face.

He sighed. "Keynes told me. Obviously. He *did* say not to tell anyone..."

"But you blabbed anyway? Jesus, man, you're sixty years old, and you haven't learned to keep your mouth shut?"

Theo finally lowered the paper, his eyes narrowed. "Aria. I am *not* sixty."

"Whatever. You're supposed to be the mature one in this group!"

"Jennifer is my wife," he sighed. "I don't hide things from my wife."

I always want to be honest with you, agapi mou.

Ruthlessly, she shoved that traitorous memory aside—and shoved her heart aside too, since it couldn't be trusted. Since it clenched every time she remembered that accented voice feeding her sweet bullshit, those gorgeous eyes lying to her.

"Well, what the fuck is Keynes's excuse?" she huffed. "You're not *his* husband."

"If platonic marriage existed," Theo said reasonably, "I would be."

"Piss off."

Jen rubbed a soothing hand over Aria's back. "It's really not that big a deal, love. I understand why you kept it to yourself.

And God, I was relieved when I found out!" She gave an airy little laugh. "I mean, at first I thought you'd really fallen for some random stranger—" Her sentence cut off abruptly, but Aria had known Jen for almost twenty years. She knew what her best friend had been about to say.

Again. I thought you'd fallen for some random stranger again.

Fuck.

This time, when the tears returned, they weren't the kind she could hide with a hug and a surreptitious swipe of her eyes. This time, they ripped her apart.

"She came home early, and now she won't stop crying! I said *crying*. Yes!" Theo was trying to be quiet, she could tell. But when he got really angry, his voice sort of expanded like a balloon. It floated in from the hallway, reaching Aria's ears without trouble.

She was alone in the living room, sobbing silently now, but the lack of sound didn't make it any less embarrassing. Jen had run off for tea. Theo had run off to ring, Aria assumed, Keynes.

"You better call that motherfucker and find out what the hell he did. I know. I *know*. Call me back."

He returned a second later with an expression of polite concern. "Well," he said, his awkward tone a world away from the whip-sharp words she'd just heard. "You seem... better."

Less hysterical, he meant. She was saved from drumming up a reply when Jen bustled into the room with a mug in each hand. She speared her husband with a glare and ordered, "Out."

Theo didn't need to be told twice.

Once he was gone, Jen turned a determinedly bright smile on Aria. "Tea!" she said, thrusting a cup into Aria's hand. Kind of like you'd thrust food at a wild animal before backing away slowly.

Aria stared glumly into the milky brown liquid. Now, the inquisition would begin.

"There," Jen said primly, sitting down. "That's better. No more tears, or your eyes will go all puffy."

"You can't appeal to my vanity right now," Aria lied. "I am desolate and despondent. I wouldn't care if my eyebrows fell off."

"Well, of course you wouldn't. You could microblade new ones for yourself."

She huffed out a resentful chuckle. "Stop making me laugh when my chest hurts."

"But that's what I'm for," Jen said softly. "Now. Do you want to tell me what happened?"

A fresh wave of despair hit Aria like a brick, completely without warning. Suddenly choking back yet *more* tears, she put down her tea and asked, "Why do you even bother with me? How many times have you had to sit around, listening to me cry over some guy like it's the first time I've been fucked over?"

Jen frowned, rolling her lips inwards. "Honey. It doesn't matter. You're my best friend and I want to be here for you. Always. And no matter how many times you get hurt, you have the right to feel that pain as if it's brand new. There's no cap on feelings." She put a hand on Aria's shoulder. "Please tell me you know that."

"Sure," Aria sniffed. "I know that. Logically. I used to tell myself that all the time. Like, yes, this guy hurt me or that guy lied, and yes, I could've seen it coming, but I'm not to blame! They're responsible for their actions and blah blah blah. But Jen, how many times can the same thing happen to me before I figure out the common denominator? I..." Her voice cracked, her vision blurring with tears. Christ, she must be so dehydrated by now. "I throw myself into relationships because I want someone to love, and I want someone to love me. But that's not okay. Look what happened last time!"

Her final sentence, the words she'd been desperate to say all along, burst out almost violently. They were so loud, they seemed to echo around the room. Jen jerked back as if she'd been hit, her mouth forming a little 'O' for a moment. But then, as always, she rallied.

"Aria Granger. Please tell me you are not still freaking out over that thing with Simon."

"Of course, I am, Jenny! I know I'm not allowed to feel guilty." Shout out to Dr. Browne, therapist extraordinaire. "But I do know that if I didn't *need* to be with someone, Simon wouldn't have been able to use me. Because I wouldn't have given him the time of day. What does it say about me, that I can fall for someone I don't even like? Nothing good, no matter which way you spin it. I know that.

"So, I decided, if I can't choose carefully, no more men! None at all! That makes sense, right? Only I fucked up. With Nik, I fucked up. Because I thought it was different, and I thought it was real, and that I wanted him—not just someone, *him*. So, I let myself try again. And I fell for someone's bullshit, *again*. I probably wanted to fall for it. I'm on some twisted self-sabotage kick where I throw myself at manipulative dickheads—"

"Wait, wait, wait," Jen said, holding up a hand. "Nik, the guy you were fake-dating? What happened?"

So, Aria told her. Aria told her everything. And at the end of the most disjointed, teary, self-pitying speech of her life, she looked up to find her best friend frowning at the wall like it held the secrets of the cosmos.

After a slight pause, Jen said, "There are a couple of things I need to say."

"O...kay?"

"First of all, Nik *is* a dickhead."

Aria laughed and accidentally blew a snot bubble. A *snot bubble*. Would these indignities never end?

"Nice," Jen said dryly.

"I told you to stop making me laugh."

"My wit is too powerful to contain, unfortunately."

Aria rolled her eyes and reached for the tissues.

"The second thing I want to say," Jen went on, "is that I understand why you're doubting yourself. Because you've definitely made some unhealthy relationship choices. I can't lie, I was glad when you stopped wifing any guy with functioning private parts, but not because I think there's something wrong with you. I think you're amazing. You love so easily."

Aria grimaced.

"That's not a bad thing! That's a gift. I've always been so jealous of you. It's like you don't have a well that can run dry, you don't have a barrier or a limit. You just love and love and love, and it never runs out, and you're never afraid. Sometimes people take advantage of you, but that is not your fault—no matter how many times it happens." Aria opened her mouth to protest, but Jen held up a hand and speared her with a look. "I don't care. It is *not your fault*. Everyone wants love, and you've got a lake of it. The people who know they don't deserve it will always be first in line, because they're thirsty. And they know how to play you, because you're too sweet to think the way they do. Like, you cannot comprehend their evil." Aria winced as Jen tapped her on the forehead. "You have a mind of hearts and flowers."

"No offence, but that is complete bullshit. I am not *sweet*."

"You are. You're like a loyal Alsatian. You will maul someone if necessary, but it's always out of love. I just wish you'd protect yourself as much as you protect everyone else."

Jen paused. "Although, it sounds like you've started to. And, while I approve wholeheartedly, I do have one last point to make."

Wariness settled over Aria. She picked up her mug of tea and took a fortifying sip. "What?"

"Like I said, Nik *is* a dick... but..."

"I don't like that *but,* Jen."

"*But,* you really like him. And he loves you."

Aria shook her head jerkily. "No. He doesn't. He—he lied to me—"

"I'm not saying you should trust him, but let's just pretend—for argument's sake—that everything he's told you is true. If you look at it *that* way, the story goes something like this: raging man-slut with zero relationship experience falls in love at first sight, doesn't know how to cope with his feelings, and cooks up a desperate plot to keep the object of his affections in his life. Gives her ridiculous amounts of money and takes her on a truly excellent holiday. Makes her happy, treats her well, bestows many orgasms, admits he loves her and comes clean about everything." Jen paused. "I don't know, Ari. Does he sound like a dick? Yes. Completely. Does he sound like an evil, manipulative scumbag? Not exactly."

"So, the best-case scenario," Aria said frostily, "is that he's a non-evil, slightly manipulative dick."

"Do you think he manipulated you into liking him?"

"Yes!"

"How?"

Aria stared at her friend. Jen was usually so smart, and yet, all of a sudden, she had become unbelievably ditsy. "He *lied* to me, so I'd spend a week pretending to be his girlfriend."

"Okay. But if that whole fake-girlfriend thing had been legit, do you think you'd have fallen for him anyway?"

"I—yes? I don't know. Probably? Well, fuck, yes, definitely. But it doesn't matter, because it *wasn't* legit."

"Right. He manipulated you into being around him. The thing is, though, it doesn't sound like he manipulated you into *liking* him. Unless you think he was fake the whole time—like, he put on some act to make you fall for him. Or he hid some fundamental part of himself that would've changed everything."

Aria forced hot tea past her cold lips. It landed with a sickening slosh in her belly. "No. No. I don't think he did that."

"Okay," Jen said softly. "So, however you feel about him, or felt, before he told you the truth... that's real. And if you really did care about him, maybe—*maybe*—you should consider giving him a chance to make it up to you."

Aria thought about that for a second. She really, really did. But her mind threw up a single answer, undeniable as a brick wall. "I can't. I just can't."

Jen gave her a sad smile. "Okay, honey. That's okay. It *was* a rather big lie."

But it wasn't Nik's lie that kept Aria awake that night, her stomach roiling and tears rolling down her cheeks. She barely thought about the lie at all.

Two images kept her up, flashing back and forth in her mind until they seemed to blur together. The look on Nik's face, when she'd told him she was leaving—as if his heart had broken and his world had ended.

And the look on Simon's, when he'd put a gun to her best friend's head.

Chapter 11

Good Luck, Mate

"What the fuck did you do to Aria?"

The sound of that name, even in Keynes's clipped tones, forced a flutter out of Nik's miserable heart. Clearly, his heart didn't quite understand the situation they were in. *Everything is fucked. We are doomed. And Aria doesn't care if you flutter for her. So chill the fuck out.*

"I fell in love with her," he said dully, staring up at the night sky. Nik should be with his friends on the last night out of the week—or at least in bed, getting ready to leave tomorrow. Instead, he'd brushed off Varo and Kieran's concern, ignored G's pointed questions, and spent the night alone in the garden, lying in the grass.

The bugs were eating him alive, but he didn't really give a shit right now.

"You fell in love with her," Keynes snorted. "Right. Okay. What country will you be in tomorrow?"

"I have no idea. Why?"

"I'd like to know your general location, so I can fly over and beat the shit out of you."

"I'll text you hourly updates."

"Thanks." Keynes sighed. "Nik, what the fuck? I never would've let you pull this weird fake girlfriend thing if I thought you'd hurt Aria. I told her you were an okay guy!"

"Well, you were wrong. I'm a piece of shit."

"Will you stop talking bollocks and say something that actually makes sense? What the hell *happened?*"

Nik ran a hand over his face. He'd never been so fucking tired in his life.

And yet, he knew he wouldn't sleep if he tried.

"That night at the hotel," he said. "When I kissed her. I... fuck, Keynes, I don't know what happened. I just knew I needed her. Forever. But then I found her the next morning, and she didn't want anything to do with me." He laughed. "I didn't ask her out. It hadn't occurred to her that I was going to. She thought I wanted her to get rid of people for me, like she did with Melissa. So, I went along with it."

"You hired her," Keynes said slowly. "To be your fake girlfriend. Because you wanted..."

"A chance. That's all. I wanted us to get to know each other, but things just happened. And then we were actually together—"

"Aria doesn't date anymore."

"Yeah, I know. She said something about that. But I guess she changed her mind. So, I told her I love her."

Keynes gave a derisive snort. "Nice one, Romeo. How'd that go?"

"It was fine. She was dealing with it. But then I told her the rest."

There was a pause. Then Keynes said flatly, "You tricked her into faking a relationship with you, made that relationship real, told her you love her, then revealed that, surprise! The whole thing was built on your aforementioned machinations."

Well, fuck. That sounded almost as bad as the way Aria had

put it. "I know the whole thing was reckless and ridiculous and selfish—"

"Did you tell her that?"

Nik winced. "Not exactly. I froze. I knew she was going to leave me, and I froze."

"Of course you did," Keynes drawled. "You spoiled man-baby."

Nik supposed he should protest that statement, only it felt pretty accurate.

"You know what? Don't bother texting updates. I don't need to hit you. Because if you're actually in love with Aria, you're going to be hurting for a very long time."

Even though Nik had thought as much, those words turned his stomach to lead. "You don't think she'll forgive me?"

"No," Keynes said grimly. "I don't."

The next few days didn't go so well for Nik.

Actually, that was an outrageous understatement. The next few days were hell.

It took him precisely one night of wallowing to remember that he was Nikolas Christou and giving up was not in his vocabulary. There was no way—absolutely none—that he was letting the love of his life just walk away from him. Even if he was the one who'd pushed her.

Of course, after that invigorating realisation, he hit a wall. The problem was, Nik couldn't see any way to reach out that wouldn't make things a thousand times worse.

Aria had told him pretty fucking clearly that she didn't want to be near him. She hadn't even let him drive her to the airport. She'd almost seemed afraid of him. And he could see now, after looking at the situation from angles other than his own self-centred, lovesick perspective, that she'd be well within her rights to think of him as a manipulative creep.

Manipulative creeps generally did not endear themselves via further harassment.

Over the days that followed their separation, Nik went home—not back to La Christou, where his family would demand to know what the hell was wrong with him, but to his flat in England. There, he spent his time thinking about Aria, mooning over Aria, and fantasising about accidentally bumping into Aria in the local Tesco (which was impossible, since he knew she lived miles away). All he wanted was to speak to her, to see her, to get on his knees and tell her he'd do anything to regain her trust. But if he came within fifty feet of her without permission, she might just call the police. And Nik believed that would be counterproductive to his aim.

He was making breakfast on the third day—buttering a bagel because it somehow reminded him of her—when the idea struck. It was obvious, really, wasn't it? He couldn't go to her, but he could make it as easy as possible for her to come to him.

She's not going to come to you. She hates you. She'll never forgive you.

Nik flicked that voice away like the gnat it was. He hadn't studied sports psychology for years just to let negative thoughts colonise his thinking and fuck up his game.

If he gave Aria everything she'd need to get in touch, and maybe apologised again—in a way that didn't put any pressure on her—she'd have time to work through her feelings. *She* could decide if she wanted to see him. And if she did, she would. And if she didn't...

Well, if she didn't, he'd have to leave her the fuck alone, wouldn't he? Even if the thought cast a film of grey over his life, his future, his *everything*. He couldn't push her; he'd already pushed her enough. He'd pushed their entire relationship into being, as if she were some kind of doll and he was the puppet master. And that wasn't how he wanted them to be. It wasn't who *he* wanted to be.

So, he'd wait. He'd wait for her. Even if it took a fucking century. Even if she never came at all.

Abandoning his bagel, Nik found his phone and brought up Keynes's number.

I need you to send this to Aria. Please send exactly this? Okay? Please. It's important.

I'm sorry. I'd find you and tell you exactly how sorry I am, but I don't think you'd want me to do that. I won't contact you again— directly or indirectly—unless you ask me to. If you don't want to now, but you do later, that's cool. Even if 'later' winds up being 2067.

If you need to talk, or you just fancy sending me a bag of dog shit, here's my address. Also, the hotel's address, in case you want to tell my mother what a dick I am. That would be excellent revenge, because she would beat me with a spoon, and those things hurt. While we're at it, here's my number, my email (which you already have) and every social media account I've ever made. I will check those every day, just in case. Even if it halves my productivity and makes me want to claw my eyes out simultaneously.

I know I fucked up. I know I lied. But everything else between us, from the first email I sent you to this message, is 100% real to me. I wasn't trying to trick you into something you didn't want to give. I didn't expect things to happen the way they did. I just loved you. I love you now. I wanted to be around you and I was incredibly selfish about it. I'm sorry. I will never be sorry enough. But I am sorry.

Yours faithfully,

Nik.

A few moments later, his phone buzzed.

Good luck, mate.

Aria thought she'd finally gotten the tears out of her system when she woke up to a text message from Keynes. Or rather, from Nik. Whatever she called it, its effect was the same.

She sat on the edge of her bed and stared at her phone and cried some more.

God, she was so bored of crying. But at least her outbursts remained varied and exciting, right? Over the past few days, she'd cried over betrayal; then bagels; then her tan lines, which reminded her of things best forgotten; and finally, her sox, which was forever ruined. And not just because she'd sat on it.

Now she was crying over Nik's message. Because, as she read the words, she could hear his voice—all cockiness gone, his tone soft and hesitant, the way it got when he was nervous.

He'd been nervous, sometimes. With her.

And once she remembered that, she remembered a thousand other things too, all of them jostling for attention, desperate to be the main cause of today's tears. Nik's smile, sometimes sweet, sometimes wicked, always provoking. Nik's constant humour, his warm, easy affection and his recklessness. She threw the phone onto the bed and slapped her hands over her eyes as if that would stop the memories, but of course it didn't.

She loved him. She loved him more than she'd ever loved anyone. She didn't know what to *do* with all this love. She was drowning in it, but the only thing that scared her about that was...

Well. Nik wasn't there to drown in it with her.

Aria stared at her hands for a moment and realised they were shaking. Then she crawled across the bed, picked up the phone she'd thrown, and called Jen.

"Hey, love. What's up?"

"Do you trust me?" The question sounded abrupt and slightly rough, a little too urgent, but that was okay. It reflected the way she felt right now.

There was a slight pause before Jen laughed, "Well, good morning! Of course I trust you."

"Even though I..." No. Aria stopped, shaking her head. She wasn't going to ask about Simon. Jen had told her the answer often enough, and it was time to start believing in it.

Even if she had to fake it before she genuinely reached that point.

"Okay. Okay." Aria took a deep breath. "Because I don't know if I should trust myself. Like, if I should believe in my own feelings or—or be wary."

"Oh, honey," Jen sighed. "I know what you mean. I know exactly what you mean."

"Do you?"

"Well, there were a lot of times, with Theo, when I wondered if I was making bad decisions. I mean, when we got together, he was my boss."

Aria nodded. At the time, she'd kind of thought Jen was making bad decisions too. Obviously, she hadn't *said* anything—but she'd been suspicious of the older, wealthy guy who held so much power over her best friend. She'd expected everything to end in tears.

And now they were married. Sometimes, she supposed, things did work out. Sometimes, people really just wanted to love you.

"Even when he proposed," Jen was saying, "I kind of wondered what the fuck I was thinking. All I knew was that I loved him, and I believed in us. And sometimes I wondered if love was a trustworthy emotion. But you know what? I think it's worth the risk."

Aria nodded slowly as her mind worked through those words. "Okay. Um... thank you."

"Do you want to talk about anything?"

"No, no. I think I'm good."

"Okay, love."

Aria put down the phone and let her messy thoughts sit for a while. Or tried to. She went about her day, looking into properties for the tattoo shop—which, yes, she was still going to do. She supposed some women might send back all that money as a point of principle. Frankly, the mere idea made Aria hysterical with laughter. She felt more inclined to demand a bonus for the way he'd fucked her over, but she wouldn't push her luck.

That thought made her imagine Nik's reaction, though. He'd laugh and argue just for the sake of it, that teasing smile on his face—but in the end he'd agree anyway, because he had this weird idea that she was smarter than him.

By the time night fell and Aria was back in bed, she'd made her decision. She opened up the thread of emails they'd begun weeks ago and sent another.

I still don't trust you.

Then she rolled over and went to sleep.

Chapter 12

Must Be My Influence

The next day Aria woke up to a reply that had arrived exactly three minutes after her email.

It's a weird feeling, to be this upset over a message but this fucking ecstatic that it came at all. I know you don't trust me, and I understand why. Can I try my best to fix it?

Aria's tongue snuck out to toy with her lip ring as she considered her response. Finally, she typed out:

You can send me shitty Vines, if you want. And anything else that will make me laugh. I don't think I can deal with heavy conversations.

She didn't know how he'd respond to that. After all, she hadn't really answered his question. She hadn't given him a chance to do or get what he wanted. And yet, she was barely surprised when he replied with exactly what she'd asked for. No further questions, no probing remarks, just a series of videos that made her laugh. He kept it up throughout the day, even though she didn't reply; one at lunch, another around dinner, another just before she went to bed.

And then he did it the next day. And the next day. And the next.

By the fifth day, the urge to reply was so strong that she stopped trying to fight it. What was the point, after all? Why was she denying herself the great luxury of a fucking email exchange?

For the first time since she'd asked him to make her laugh, Aria typed out a message to Nik.

"Well, then." Lila Jones, British footballing legend, looked around the table of suits. "I don't know about all of you, but I think we definitely have space for Mr. Christou within the foundation."

The swell of pleasure in Nik's chest was muted, like a lot of his feelings recently—but it was undeniably there. And it grew in intensity as the rest of the room nodded, murmuring their agreement and flashing welcoming smiles. Satisfaction bloomed. He'd decided that since he had enough money—*more* than enough—he didn't need to look for work as a coach or a manager. Instead, he wanted to focus on philanthropic pursuits. To help people. He'd be working with Lila's charity, which focused on making football training accessible to disadvantaged girls—but it had occurred to him that, when he knew enough, he could also choose a cause back home.

He remembered Aria telling him that he could do anything. Would it be too much to let her know that he was doing this? Probably. He was excited, and she was the person he wanted to blurt out all his excitement to, but it wouldn't make her laugh. He was supposed to be making her laugh.

Maybe he'd get the chance to tell her eventually.

It was that *maybe*, on top of his success at the meeting,

that had Nik leaving the foundation's offices with a grin on his face and a bounce in his step. He pulled out his phone to text Varo.

And saw a notification he hadn't expected, but desperately wanted. One that took his tentative happiness, strapped a rocket to it, and sent it soaring across the sky like a comet.

Aria had finally replied.

Your taste in Vines has improved since the last time we emailed. Must be my influence.

His grin was so wide, it felt like he might break his own face. He almost dropped the phone in his haste to reply.

Definitely. I'd say you've improved a lot of things about me.

He paced the street as he waited for her answer, ignoring his parked car. He couldn't sit in a confined space right now. Not when bright, burning hope was bursting inside him. He traced his own footsteps across the tarmac five times before his phone vibrated in his hand.

Suck-up. How are you?

Right now, I'm very good. Excellent. Fantastic. Never better. How are you? How are things going with the shop?

I'm okay. They're good, actually. I'm looking at locations and enjoying being rich. Although 350k doesn't go as far as I thought it would. Is that why you guys hoard wealth?

Nik didn't bother holding back his laughter. He started to type out 'I miss you', then shook his head and deleted it.

Maybe. But you might be interested to know that my latest occupation is unpaid.

You're being circumspect to pique my interest. I know your games.

He would be worried about that last email, except she followed it up with a winking emoji. An emoji! That little yellow face almost gave him heart failure. She was... sharing emotions? Tiny, graphic emotions. With him. Positive ones, even. All of a sudden, every word he typed seemed like the word that could potentially ruin unbelievable progress. The pressure got so great that in the end, Nik had to sit on the curb, right there in the street, and pull himself together.

Guilty as charged. But I will happily write you a lengthy essay on the meeting I just had if that's what you want. Say the word.

An essay might be a bit much. Why don't I just call you?

Nik wasn't sure what he said in response. *Jesus fuck yes, please call me,* perhaps. It was all a bit of a blur. And then his phone was ringing, and he was practically cracking the screen in his rush to answer. "Hello?"

The sound of her voice washed over him like an ocean wave, powerful and perfect. "Hi."

"How are you?"

"Didn't we already cover that?" He could hear her smiling. She was smiling. For him. Fuck, his palms were sweating. He was going to tell her so—but wait, no, he didn't want to pour his feelings all over her and make her feel responsible for them. This whole thing was supposed to be low-pressure, all her, no bullshit from his end.

So, he just laughed and said, "Yeah. Yeah, we did. I just—I want to know you're good, that's all."

"I'm good," she answered softly. "So, tell me about this mysterious *occupation.*"

Nik sat on the street and told Aria everything he knew,

everything he'd hoped for, and everything he'd soon be a part of. To his everlasting relief, she actually seemed pleased. Impressed, even. She told him about her plans for the shop, the progress she'd made, and seemed happy when he was interested. She asked how his tattoo was healing. She said...

She said, out of nowhere, "God, Nik, I missed your voice."

At which point, he was almost delirious with happiness. "You did? What does that—? Wait, no, you don't have to answer that. I just—"

"I haven't forgiven you." The words fell on his fledgling hope like bricks. But hope was a tough little fucker. It was still alive under there; he could feel it, bright and strong. Then she sighed and said, "No, that's not right. I think I have forgiven you. I just, I'm struggling to... well. It's all part of a very long story."

"You know you can tell me anything," he said, because the hollow dip in her voice made him think that this 'long story' was something she needed to release. He wanted to be the one who helped her do it. He wanted all her stories, long and short. "Anytime, anywhere. I'm in the U.K., you know."

"You are?"

"Yeah. Not because of you." *Technically.* "I still live here. When I'm not at home, I mean." God, he was talking too much.

"Well, okay. Maybe we could hang out. At some point. Eventually."

Never had such stilted, half-hearted words sounded sweeter to Nik's ears. "I would love that. I would really fucking love that."

"Okay. Cool. Um... I have to go."

"Alright, sweetheart." Fuck. He hadn't meant to say that.

But she didn't mention it. "Bye, Nik."

"Goodbye."

When the call ended, Nik celebrated harder in his suit and tie, in front of baffled pedestrians, than he ever had for any goal.

Two weeks later, Nikolas Christou found himself sitting in a restaurant with the love of his life.

She looked amazing, he assumed. He wasn't completely sure. He couldn't see her very well, what with the stars in his eyes. But he heard her just fine, when she asked suddenly, "Have you had sex since I last saw you?"

Nik frowned, the stars falling away with a blink. And, yes, she *did* look amazing—even though she was eyeing him suspiciously. Her hair was shorter with ice blue streaks, her lips shone with that gloss he loved so much, and her curves were clad in a tiny, lime-green dress. She stood out like a beacon in a fancy restaurant full of plain people in plainer clothes.

"No," Nik said finally. "Of course I haven't."

"Why 'of course'?"

He shrugged. "You left me. I never left you."

She shook her head and laughed softly, turning her gaze to the menu. "How very Nik of you."

"What?"

"You know what you want out of life, don't you?"

He hadn't, actually. Not until he met her.

Aria's gaze softened, her mouth twisting slightly. "I'm sorry. It just kind of hit me, when I saw you, that you might have... I don't know."

Nik smiled. He wanted to grin like a five-year-old and dance on the table because, apparently, she was hypothetically jealous. But he limited himself to that smile and said, "Turns out I'm great at saying no when I have a reason."

"I'm a reason?"

The Fake Boyfriend Fiasco

"Aria. I love you."

The tip of her tongue slid out to nudge at her lip ring. She held his gaze for a second before her eyes fluttered away like butterflies, too fast to catch. "Why am I staring at wine? Fuck wine. I need food."

He laughed. He teased her. She teased him right back. And just like that, it was as if nothing had happened, as if he'd never fucked up and she'd never left, and they were just... *them.* Together. The way they were meant to be.

Through the starter and the main course, they managed to skirt around the elephant in the room. It was like a dance, as if the melody of their laughter and the beat of their back-and-forth kept them on track, showing their feet where to go.

But then, just after they ordered dessert, Aria's mouth tightened. Her whiskey eyes became shadowed, her shoulders rigid, and he knew before she said a word that they were about to talk. To *Talk,* actually. Capital T.

He'd been waiting for this—for the chance to discuss what had happened between them, to really apologise, to explain what had been going through his head. But he was dreading it, too, because she'd said that she wanted to tell him something. And he had a feeling that this *something* might be responsible for the haunted look that came over her every so often. He had a feeling that someone had hurt her.

And that he'd made it worse.

"I told you, at one point, that I wasn't really dating," she said. Her words held the tone of a lengthy speech, an introduction rather than a casual comment, so he nodded wordlessly, not wanting to interrupt. "Well..." She huffed out a long, slow breath. And then, all at once, a rapid stream of words fell from her lips. "Well, I decided to avoid men because I can't trust myself with relationships, because I just, you know, I'm in them just to be in them, which is fine until it starts to hurt people, and

177

it started to hurt people, because I dated this one guy last year and he turned out to be a murderous stalker and he kidnapped Jen and she nearly died and he blew his own hand off and—"

Nik held up a hand. "Stop."

She stopped.

He hadn't planned on touching her tonight, but he reached across the table and caught her shaking fingers with his own. "Are you okay?"

Slowly, her laboured breaths calmed. "I'm fine. I'm just nervous."

"What are you nervous about?"

"I've only really talked about this with my therapist."

Nik took a deep breath and savoured the cool air that flooded his lungs. It helped with his anger, his worry, his fear— none of which would be useful to her now. "Okay. Well, let me make sure I understand. You were seeing someone."

"Yes."

"And he kidnapped your best friend."

"Yes!"

"And did *what* to his hand?"

She shifted in her seat. "He had a gun. And there was, like, a police stand-off, but when he pulled the trigger, it kind of back-fired... The police said it was homemade, or something. Did you know you can make guns? I didn't know that."

Nik swallowed. "Was she okay?"

"Ah, well, she turned out to be pretty good in a crisis. She stabbed him. With a screwdriver. So, when he managed to fire the gun, she was kind of out of range, and then it sort of blew up, and he lost his hand, and she..." Aria's hand fluttered up to the side of her face. "She's got these scars. I suppose she's okay, now. She seems fine."

"And when was this?"

"Ummm... November."

Nik's throat went dry. *Less than a year ago.*

"So, you see," she said, "I'm thinking that... well, that I might have overreacted a little bit. With you. Because I felt like every guy was hiding some dangerous side to their personality, and I was too desperate for affection to figure it out—"

"Aria, you didn't overreact." His grip on her hand tightened, as if he could push his words into her skin as well as telling her out loud. "Never think you overreacted. You felt how you felt, and you behaved accordingly. And if me lying hit you even harder because of your past... Well, I shouldn't have lied at all. If I'd acted right, you wouldn't have a reason to be upset. That's *my* fault. It's all my fault. Okay?"

She nodded slowly. "Okay." And then, after a moment, a tentative smile lit up her face. "I mean, obviously it's your fault. Everything's your fault. Because you suck."

"Definitely," he agreed, his voice solemn.

"I mean, global warming, the bees—"

"Well, maybe not that stuff."

"The deterioration of Topshop's quality—"

"I don't actually think—"

"Why are you arguing with me?" She grinned. "Aren't you supposed to be winning me back?"

Nik froze. "*Can* I win you back?"

She gave a studied shrug. "I don't know. Maybe if you tried really hard."

"I'm prepared to try hard. The hardest."

"And maybe if you explain what the fuck you thought you were doing, coming up with that bullshit plan."

Nik sighed and ran a hand through his hair. "Yes. *Yes.* I would love to explain that."

"Well, go on." She cocked her head mockingly, a little smile playing about her lips. But she hadn't pulled her hand from his. She was holding on to him.

Please, don't let go.

"First, I want to apologise for not apologising enough at the time. I don't think I took it as seriously as I should have. I didn't expect you to be that upset, because, honestly, I was thoughtless. I saw it all from my own perspective. *I knew I didn't want to hurt you, I knew I loved you, I knew my intentions—but you didn't. So, I'm sorry.*"

She nodded. "Right. And, um... What were your intentions?"

The fact that she even cared had him ready to pass out in relief. Because intentions didn't matter half as much as actual, concrete results, and the results of his actions had been hurting her. Yet she was giving him the chance to tell her all of this, anyway.

"I love you," he said. "Do you mind me saying that?"

She smiled. "You can continue. If you must."

"Sometimes it just kind of comes out."

"I am extremely loveable, so I understand."

He grinned. "Of course, you do. Well, as far as intentions go —I thought you'd get to know me, and then you'd be more open to seeing me again. I hoped that maybe we'd be friends. And I wanted to be around you, because I had this—this need, like I couldn't let you out of my sight before I knew more about you. Only, I *never* knew enough about you. I found out how you sleep and wondered what you eat when you're sick. You told me a story about your past and I wanted to see all your baby pictures. I want every part of you. And I've never felt like that before, so I fucked up. But if you let me, I'd really love to never, ever fuck up again."

A slow smile spread over her face throughout his speech, as steady and warm as the hope swelling in his heart. Still, she arched a brow and murmured, "I'm pretty sure you'll fuck up again. Humans do that."

"True," he admitted. "But I'll never lie to you. I'll never hide anything from you. I'll never put myself before you."

Her smile widened into a grin. "That sounds okay."

"It does?"

"It does."

"So..."

"So," she said, her eyes lighting up as dessert arrived. "This is our first date."

Which was when Nik realised that, all this time, there'd been an entire level of happiness he'd never reached before. And now here he was, on top of the world, feeling it.

Because of her.

"Now," Nik began as they wandered down the moonlit street. "How are you getting home?"

Aria swung her little handbag and tried, fruitlessly, to calm her grin. She was just so full of joy, she might burst. Like a balloon. A happy, happy balloon. "I don't know. Bus, maybe."

He looked up sharply, clearly appalled. Even horrified, he was handsome as fuck. She'd spent the whole meal half-mesmerised by his gorgeous bloody face. The rest of her attention had been taken up by the yearning in his eyes when he looked at her, the tenderness in his voice when they spoke, the way he ran those big, capable hands through his hair as he considered his words.

She'd wondered, during their time apart, if she'd imagined how things were between them. If she'd seen him through the veil of a holiday romance, falling for a man she'd half-imagined instead of the man who actually existed. But tonight cemented what she'd already figured out over the past couple of weeks: she adored him. She more than adored him. He was everything she'd never thought to want. She didn't have to bend and twist the idea of him to make them fit; she didn't have to hide anything about herself or fabricate new parts for them to work.

They just *were*. And it was so natural, she couldn't stop it even if she'd tried.

"Let me take you home," he frowned. He seemed genuinely concerned by the idea of her taking the bus. Bless.

But, as Aria prepared to refuse, something hit her like a bolt of lightning: She could say yes.

Her lips would *allow* her to say yes, if she wanted. She wouldn't stand frozen, terrified by the idea of giving him her address. She wouldn't hesitate as she got into his car, thinking of the man who'd tied her friend up in the back of his van.

She could say yes.

And the thought was so freeing, so impossibly wonderful, that she did it. She said, "Okay." Once that word was out, she said more, unable to stop herself. "I love you, Nik. You're going to be so fucking smug about it, but I do."

He stopped in his tracks, shock written all over his face. "Are you serious?"

"Like I'd give you a reason to crow if I wasn't."

"You—I—Aria—"

"What?"

He stood for a moment as if he were malfunctioning, like his fuses had blown or something. Then, all at once, he wrapped his arms around her and hauled her up against his chest, spinning them both in circles.

Finally, after she shrieked and slapped at his shoulder and tried to pretend she wasn't thoroughly enjoying herself, Nik put her down again. But he didn't let her go. Instead, his hands cradled her face as if she were the most precious thing he'd ever held.

"I love you so fucking much," he grinned. "I want to kiss you. Can I kiss you?"

"You'd better."

And he did. God, he did. His mouth teased hers at first, the tip of his tongue tracing the seam of her lips, making her gasp and rise up for more. When the heat pooling between her thighs became unbearable, when she clutched at his strong arms and felt her knees weaken, he finally gave her what she needed. His lips moved over hers, each kiss long and slow, as if he were trying to tell her something. To show her something. To give her a part of himself.

So she threaded her fingers through his hair, and kissed him right back, and gave him her heart.

A Soft and Mushy Epilogue

Decades Later

"**M**um. Dad. I have fallen in love."

Aria didn't look up from her sketchbook. "That's nice, darling."

She expected her husband to be similarly underwhelmed; after all, their eldest daughter said the same thing every other month. Helen reminded Aria of the way she'd been in her younger years, if far less self-destructive. The child—woman, now—had an excess of love and no qualms about sharing it.

So, when Nik grabbed the TV remote and turned off the football, Aria was surprised, to say the least. She finally looked up to find her husband staring at their firstborn with a rather disconcerting expression.

Helen stared right back, her shoulders set as if awaiting some sort of military inspection. "I'm telling you because I will be needing giagiá's ring," she said, "and I know it's in the safety deposit right now."

Aria's jaw dropped. "Honey... Grandma's ring? I didn't even know you were seeing anyone." She looked over at Nik, but for once he didn't join her in baffled eye contact. He was still staring at their daughter, giving Aria a perfect view of the stripes of silver at his temples and the lines bracketing his narrowed eyes.

"I'm not," Helen said. "I mean, we're not together. Yet. She's a PhD student at the university. I, ah, saw her at a lab the other day." Helen's cheeks darkened. "Oh, come on, Ma, don't look at me like that."

With great difficulty, Aria toned down her blatant astonishment. "You want grandma's ring for a girl you *saw* at a *lab* the *other day?*"

Before Helen could reply, Nik spoke suddenly. "I'll get it tomorrow."

Aria's head whipped around to her husband. "You'll *what?*"

"Thanks, Dad." Helen left the room nonchalantly, as if she hadn't just turned her mother's world upside down.

Aria blinked helplessly at Nik. "Am I missing something?"

He pulled her sketchbook gently from her hands before hauling her into his lap. She huffed, fidgeting as if this weren't the most comfortable place in the world. He held her tight, as always, his hands cupping her belly, his chin resting on her shoulder. "She's in love, chrysí mou."

"She's always in bloody love."

"But some kinds are different."

"You can't possibly know—"

"Do you trust me?"

She laughed, sliding a hand over his cheek. "Oh, stop that. You know I do."

Nik pressed a kiss to her lips. "Good. Our daughter is in love. But, since she is much smarter than me, I'm sure she won't make a mess of it the way I did."

A wry smile twisting her lips, Aria shifted until she was straddling him, face-to-face. "Oh, I don't know. I think you handled things okay, in the end."

185

"Was that praise I just heard? From my lovely wife? Surely not."

"Oh, fuck off," she snorted.

"I'd rather fuck you."

"Behave."

"I'd rather not."

"Kiss me, then."

"Now that," Nik grinned, "I can do."

Bonus Content

Thank you so much for reading *The Fake Boyfriend Fiasco*.
Want more of Nik and Aria? Join my VIP newsletter for their
steamy bonus epilogue.

taliahibbert.com/viplist

Ready for another fake relationship romance? Read
on for a sneak peek at *The Princess Trap*, which features a royal
hero, a deeply unimpressed heroine, and a few dark secrets...

The Princess Trap

Cherry Neita was not the type of woman to voluntarily use stairs.

As far as she was concerned, they were inconvenient, inappropriate, and a public nuisance. Unless she was firmly strapped into a sports bra, with a bottle of Lucozade in hand, Cherry avoided physical exertion like the plague.

Which was why she had perfected the art of pushing into the queue for the lift. And her colleagues here at the Academy made it so *easy*. Bless them.

"Excuse me, gentlemen, thank you!" Cherry wiggled her way through the gaggle of men loitering in front of the building's single lift.

Why the Academy's senior leadership team was housed with the lowly administrative staff—and *why* the tower they all shared had only one lift—Cherry didn't know. She avoided wondering about it, too, because poor organisation made her skin crawl. Honestly, if they'd only consulted her during the bloody planning stages...

"Morning, Cherry, darling," beamed Jeff, the Academy's

rosy-cheeked Head of Key Stage 4. For a man who spent so much time working with teenagers, he was always remarkably cheerful. Cherry had to admire his fortitude.

"Morning, Jeff. How's—?" Her response was interrupted by a disgruntled muttering from somewhere behind her. Cherry turned to find Mike Cousins, Head of Geography, giving her a dark look. The sort of look that said, *I've been waiting here for ages. How did she get to the front of the queue?*

It was the arse-crack of bloody morning, so Cherry's mood was not the best. But cussing someone out at work for having the audacity to *look* at her would be a trifle unreasonable, so she collected the threads of her patience with great effort, and dragged her lips up from a demure smile to a full-on, charming grin. Mike blinked under the force of her dimples, then smiled back, all annoyance forgotten.

The men in this place responded to a pretty face like babies to a bottle. And she was supposed to respect them.

Sigh.

Turning back to Jeff, Cherry continued. "How's Sandra and the kids?"

"Not bad, not bad." The lift arrived with a *ding*, and Jeff stepped aside to let her walk in first. What a gentleman. "Little one's teething," he went on, "but otherwise well."

"Wonderful!"

A handful of staff members forced themselves into the lift behind Jeff and Cherry. They faced front like good little soldiers. Cherry, unembarrassed, studied her reflection in the lift's mirrored back wall. Life was too short to pretend you didn't want to check your lipstick.

"And how are you, Cherry?"

"Oh, you know." She fluffed at her hair, as though the mass of dark coils weren't springy enough already. "Same as usual."

Ding.

"Well!" Cherry turned away from her reflection with a smile. Just a small one, no dimples. She tried not to unleash them in enclosed spaces. "I'll see you later, Jeff."

"Cheerio, love." He smiled back, genuine as always. Jeff was probably the only senior member of staff who didn't make her want to be sick. He was sweet, he was honest, and he cared about the kids, so Cherry always had a kind word for him.

The rest of them could get fucked.

She stepped out of the lift and into the safety of the admin floor with relief. It was the only place at Rosewood Academy that felt like something other than a greedy, corporate pipeline.

See, once upon a time, Rosewood had been an actual school. Until a mate of the Prime Minister's with a background in private education had taken over and 'academised'—AKA *monetised*—the place. Now the kids were pumped through the system like battery hens, and woe betide anyone who fell below industry standard.

Cherry wound her way through the rows of desks and occasional offices that filled the floor, greeting colleagues as she went. She didn't bother with exaggerated wiggles and dimpled smiles up here. No-one was silly enough to fall for it, or dangerous enough to warrant her Darling Doll performance, anyway. She reached the HR office and paused, reading the sign blu-tacked to the door with a frown.

CHERRY NEITA, KEEP OUT!

With a shrug, she swept into the room.

"Oh! Cherry! What are you doing here?" Inside the office, two women huddled protectively around Cherry's desk. She struggled to place them. They were in finance, she thought... and the little, dark-haired one *might* be called Julie.

The taller of the two women looked at Cherry as if she were a rampaging bull. "Didn't you see the sign?"

"No," Cherry said blithely. "What are you doing at my desk, girls?"

Across the room, seated neatly at her own desk, Rose McCall snorted. She raised one pale, wrinkled hand to her spectacles, peering at Cherry over their half-moon lenses. "What do you *think*, darling?"

Cherry held back a sigh. It took great effort, but she managed.

"Sorry, Cherry," the tall one wheedled. "It's just that Julie and I were talking, and she—"

Cherry held up a hand. "You don't have to explain. Have I ruined the surprise?"

"A little bit," Julie admitted. "I don't know *how* you missed the sign."

"It's a mystery for the ages," murmured Rose. Cherry gave the older woman *A Look*.

"Well, anyway," Julie said. She tried for a grin, but it looked more like a wince. "Surprise!" The pair sprang apart like show girls, waving their hands towards Cherry's desk. Or rather, towards the monstrous mess they'd made of it.

Her neat and tidy workspace was covered in glitter and confetti. In the centre of the desk sat a huge, ceramic number '30' in a screaming shade of pink. As if she didn't know precisely how old she was.

God, Cherry hated birthdays. They were so... unnecessary. All that attention, and none of it under her control.

"Oh, you two," she said, pasting a coy smile onto her face. "You shouldn't have."

"Really," Rose echoed. "You shouldn't have."

The woman was a bloody nuisance. A brilliant bloody nuisance, but a nuisance all the same.

Julie's hopeful face fell. "I know you hate a fuss, but—"

"No!" Cherry said firmly. "This is lovely. I very much appreciate it. I—" she broke off as she caught sight of a little box beside the ornament. "Is that *Hotel Chocolat?*"

"Yes!" Julie said proudly.

Rose sat up straight in her chair. "Where?" she demanded, squinting across the room.

"Never you mind." Cherry stepped forward and swept up the box with a smile. "Really, ladies, thank you so much. What a lucky girl I am."

The admin staff persisted in sucking up to her purely because Rose, the Head of HR and mistress of all she surveyed, was impossible to suck up to. Usually it was rather annoying, but in this case, Cherry couldn't pretend to mind. As the girls left, looking rather pleased with themselves, she ripped open her box of chocolates.

"Don't be greedy, love." Rose stood and sauntered over, her fluid movements as deceptive as her plump, rosy cheeks. Rose McCall was, Cherry knew, sixty-seven. She appeared no older than fifty, despite her lavender-grey chignon.

"Says you," Cherry mumbled, her mouth full. But she held out the box, and didn't even complain when Rose took two truffles at once.

"I *am* sorry," Rose said conspiratorially. She perched herself on the edge of Cherry's desk. "I had no idea they were going to surprise you. Truthfully, I didn't realise anyone knew your birthday."

"Facebook," Cherry said glumly.

"Oh, yes." Rose popped a truffle into her mouth. "Well, you know I don't hold with that nonsense myself."

"I don't know," Cherry mused. "It can be annoying. But there are a lot of cat videos."

Before Rose could reply, the door to their office burst open.

Again. Really, all this human contact was a bit much for one morning.

It was Louise, one of the receptionists, all pink-cheeked and wide-eyed. "Rose!" she gasped. "Cherry! Oh, you won't believe what's happened!"

"Calm down," Rose frowned. "Are you alright?"

"No!" Louise shrieked. "I'm as likely to pass out as—" she broke off, her eyes narrowing. "Is that *Hotel Chocolat*?"

Cherry slapped the lid back onto the box. "All gone. Sorry."

"Bugger. Anyway, listen to this!"

Cherry listened. Rose listened. Louise paused dramatically.

"Come on, then," Rose finally snapped. She wasn't known for her patience.

Louise relented, her tone hushed. "There's a *man*."

Cherry looked at Rose. Rose looked at Cherry. They might work in a school—sorry, *educational academy*—but men *did* appear from time to time. True, they tended to belong to senior management rather than, say, the admin team. But they were hardly a rare sighting.

"A *man*?" Rose prompted.

"Yes." Louise nodded like a bobble-head. "A *new* man. A visitor. And he's absolutely bloody gorgeous."

Cherry leaned forward. "*Is* he, now?"

"His backside is unbelievable," Louise breathed. Her voice was reverent. Her eyes were slightly unfocused. Cherry's interest was most firmly piqued.

"And who is this man?" Rose demanded. "What's he doing here?"

Louise hesitated.

"Oh, for Christ's sake. That's all the gossip you have?"

"I'm afraid so, Rose. He's just come in, you see, and Chris fairly whisked him away..."

"Well," Rose sniffed. "You'd best get back to reception, before you miss anything else."

"You're right," the younger woman murmured, almost to herself. "He might come out again. There might be *more* of them!" She disappeared without bothering to say goodbye. As the door swung shut, Cherry wondered just *how* handsome this man could possibly be. Perhaps she could...

Don't even think about it. You're a sensible adult who does not make a fool of herself at work. You are a mature woman entering the prime of her life, not to be distracted by—

"Go and investigate, will you, darling?"

Cherry stood. "If you insist."

———

His Royal Highness Prince Magnus Ruben Ambjørn Octavian Gyldenstierne of Helgmøre—widely known as Ruben—was trying his best not to look bored. After all, contrary to popular belief, he did have *some* manners.

But he was almost certainly failing.

Still, he supposed it didn't really matter. Chris Tabary, the source of Ruben's current boredom, was so far up his own arse that he probably wouldn't notice if Ruben whipped off his trousers and threw them out the bloody window.

"After lunch," the older man droned, "we'll begin touring the new build—soon to be the *elite* branch of the Academy, for our particularly promising pupils..."

Ruben's mind, which had been in the middle of deciding how soon was too soon to leave, pounced on the word *elite* like a cat with a mouse.

"What does that mean?" he demanded, leaning forward. He could almost feel the eyes of his close guard and best friend, Hans, boring into the back of his head. Could almost hear the other man's voice: *Don't let your mouth run away with you. Again.* Clearing his throat, Ruben attempted to sound polite. "I mean—when you say 'elite', you are referring to...?"

Tabary blinked. Clearly, he was not used to being interrupted. But he collected himself in record time, clasping his slender hands together and offering what he probably thought of as a charming smile. It was a little too wide, a little too plastic, and showed far too many teeth.

"By 'elite', Your Highness—"

Ruben sighed. "Please. No titles. I assume Demetria sent you the materials?" It was a rhetorical question. Demetria *always* sent the materials.

"Ah, yes." Tabary appeared slightly unsettled by his mistake. He winced a little, his smile wavering before he dragged it back into place. "My apologies. I should say, *Mr. Ambjørn.* Here at the Academy, we pay special attention to those students identified as elite via our stratified testing system. Students are monitored throughout the term, and tested once per year—"

"Aside from the national tests, you mean?"

"Precisely. Every September, we undertake school-wide testing to ensure that our most elite intellectuals are separated from the other students."

Ruben's alarm bells were not simply ringing; they were screaming. "By testing," he said carefully, "you refer to... ah... examination? In a room?" At Tabary's slight frown, he added, "My English. You understand."

Ruben's English was perfect, courtesy of three years studying at the University of Edinburgh. But surely he must be misunderstanding here? Surely Tabary did not insist on extra testing just to create some kind of intelligence-based class system in his school?

Tabary offered a benevolent smile. "Well, yes, examinations.

The students are taken into a room and asked to complete a question paper in silence. Then we mark the papers... *et voila!*" He chuckled.

Ruben nodded along politely. Mentally, he was planning the easiest way to extract himself from this situation.

Rosewood Academy was *not* an appropriate contender for the scholarship programme he planned to create. Excessive testing was something Ruben disapproved of anyway, but sending the children that his Trust catered to—children of disadvantaged backgrounds and unique needs—to a school that openly referred to better-testing students as *elite*...

Demetria would be so smug when she found out about this. Hadn't she told him to stop accepting applicants based on nothing but social networking?

Shifting in his seat, Ruben turned to catch his bodyguard's eye. Hans stood, as always, by the door, looking dour and dangerous as ever. Ruben would give the signal, and Hans would think up some sort of excuse—

The sound of voices floated in through Tabary's office door. It was muffled, but still clear enough to distract Ruben from his plan.

"Oh! Hello..." The voice softened, trailing off into a low murmur that he couldn't quite catch. Then came another voice in response, much lower than the first. *That* was one of his guards. Who were they talking to?

"Are you alright, Mr. Ambjørn?"

Ruben turned back towards Tabary, and found the man looking at him with a frown.

"Yes, yes," Ruben said. "Just... thought I heard something."

"Oh, there's often a racket along these corridors." Tabary waved a hand. "We share the tower with the administrative staff. They roam around clucking like hens, bless them. Our girls love a gossip."

Ruben's brows shot up. *Our girls love a gossip?* The patronising little shit.

Fuck manners. He was leaving.

But, before he could make a move, there came a sharp knock at the door. He had just enough time to wonder if there was some emergency—hadn't Tabary asked not to be disturbed?—before the door opened and a hurricane swept inside.

"Chris, darling!" She tottered in on high-heels, closing the door behind her with a bump of her hips. And good Lord, what hips. "I'm *so* sorry to disturb you, but this absolutely couldn't wait."

The hurricane was a woman. A woman with laughing eyes and a heart-shaped face and a figure that could kill a man. A woman whose dark, springy curls gleamed like midnight, who had incongruously chubby cheeks and brown-sugar skin.

She sailed past Hans as if he wasn't even there, and Ruben wondered what had happened to the men stationed outside. Then he watched her hips sway as she walked, and decided they'd probably passed out at the sight of her.

"Cherry," Tabary said, frowning at her. Ruben wondered why he was calling her Cherry—a pet name?—and why he was frowning at the most beautiful woman on earth. Had the man no fucking sense? "This is a very important meeting," Tabary continued.

"Oh, I'm *so* sorry," the woman said, her tone dripping with apology. But Ruben had the strangest impression that she wasn't sorry at all. Then, for the first time since she'd come in, her eyes flitted over to his.

And he realised that *beautiful* was an understatement.

Her face was almost unnaturally perfect. For one disturbing moment he was reminded of his sister—but Sophronia's beauty was cold. So fucking cold.

This woman might burst into flame at any moment.

She slapped a stack of papers on Tabary's desk and bent at the waist, leaning over his shoulder as she pointed at something on the first page. Her cleavage, already magnificent, swelled against the neckline of her dress. Ruben reminded himself to keep breathing.

"If you could just have a look at this," she said, her voice soft. "I can't quite get a handle on it..."

Tabary's frown disappeared, and he gave the woman a look of affection. That look made Ruben's fists clench, made him grind his teeth—which was both ridiculous and inevitable. He may not know this woman, but something about her triggered a single, disturbing thought.

I have to have her.

Confusing. Surprising. He'd seen plenty of beautiful people in his time, and he'd never reacted like this. But Ruben wasn't in the habit of ignoring his instincts.

"Oh, Cherry," Tabary tutted. "Silly girl. Look here; you've mucked up the sums. That's all."

The woman put her fingers to her lips. No—she brought them to hover just over her lips, which were painted scarlet. Her eyes widened like a doe's as she gasped. "Oh, Chris! You're right. What am I like?"

Tabary rolled his eyes dramatically, a grin bursting across his narrow face. The kind of grin that weak men released when offered the chance to correct a supposedly stupid woman. His annoyance forgotten, he handed the papers back with a fond smile. "Off you go, Cherry, dear. I *am* in the middle of something."

The woman straightened up, clutching the papers to her chest. Her eyes settled on Ruben with exaggerated surprise, as if she'd only just noticed his presence. And he knew instantly that she'd orchestrated this entire thing.

"Oh, gosh," she said. "How rude of me." And then, skirting

around Tabary's desk, she stepped right up to him, held out a hand, and said: "Cherry Neita."

Cherry. Her *name* was Cherry.

Ruben stood and took her hand in his. Her skin was warm and soft, her fingers tipped with the most outrageous nails—long and pink and glittery, all studded with gems. Ridiculous. He adored them. Bowing over her hand, Ruben pressed the ghost of a kiss to her knuckles.

Then Hans, the fucker, cleared his throat. Loudly.

Oh. Right. Kissing women's hands wasn't the best way to *blend in.*

Trying not to wince, Ruben straightened up and gave her his handsomest smile. Prince Charming he was not—as the press loved to remind him—but for this woman, he'd do his best.

"Ruben Ambjørn," he replied. It wasn't a lie, he told himself. Not technically.

"Lovely to meet you," she murmured. And for a moment, her voice dipped from the light, airy tone she'd used with Chris to something low and earthy that suited her far better. Then she looked down at their hands, arching a brow—and he realised that he was still clutching her fingers like a lost child.

He should probably let go.

No, his newly animalistic mind whispered. *Never let her go.*

Hm. His mind was starting to sound like a stalker.

Ruben released her, trying not to make his reluctance obvious. "What is it you do here, Ms. Neita?" He imagined she'd make an excellent teacher. Her class wouldn't know what'd hit them.

But God, if he'd ever had a tutor like her...

"I'm in HR," she said, shattering his fantasies. "And I really should get back upstairs. *So* sorry to intrude." She turned to Tabary and flashed him a smile, wider this time—and Jesus fucking Christ, she had *dimples*. That simply wasn't fair. "See you later, Chris!"

With that, she disappeared, hips swaying beneath her tight skirt. The door swung shut behind her, and the office descended into a dazed sort of silence.

Cherry fucking Neita. Fancy that.

The Princess Trap is available now wherever books are sold.

Author's Note

I started self-publishing back in 2017 as a broke uni student living in my childhood bedroom, so it's safe to say I had The Hunger.

My first success was a boss/employee romantic suspense called *Bad for the Boss* (Jen and Theo's story), which I turned into a barely interconnected series; book 2 was *Undone by the Ex-Con* and book 3 was *Sweet on the Greek*.

That series helped me find my voice, and it turns out said voice is less 'silver fox rescues ingenue from danger' and more 'horny fools pine for each other and eat snacks'. As my career matured, I found books 1 and 2 no longer suited my catalogue, so I unpublished them.

But book 3, *Sweet on the Greek*? It was bonkers and smutty and emotional and it suited me down to the ground. So I jiggled the contents around a bit (but honestly, not a lot), polished to a high shine, and changed the title.

However, *Bad for the Boss* and *Undone by the Ex-Con* are still out of print, and likely always will be. I know! I'm sorry! The completionist in me hates it too, but trust me when I say, it's for the best.

Author's Note

If you want to stay in this world, never fear: you can grab Keynes and Griffin's story, _Work for It_, right now. It's about farming and inner demons and hate-sex in the woods.

Happy reading!

Acknowledgments

Thank you to Jennifer Scarberry for getting this book ready for publication, and being the best cheerleader an author could ask for.

Thank you to Meeghan Webster for being an epic book guardian.

Thank you to Em and Zahra for coaxing my questionable ideas and terrible first drafts into a book.

Thank you to Sam for telling me football stuff when I asked, even though you've been trying to do that for the past six years and I've been dodging you at every turn.

Thank you to Yasi and her family for all the Greek advice and for their boring breakfasts. (Bet you thought I wouldn't put that in, huh?)

And finally, thank you to Ellen Baier, patron extraordinaire. You make me smile every day, and you don't even know it.

About the Author

Talia Hibbert is a *New York Times* bestselling and award-winning author who lives in a bedroom full of books. Supposedly, there is a world beyond that room, but she has yet to drum up enough interest to investigate.

Talia writes sexy, diverse romance because marginalised people deserve joyous representation, and also because she very much enjoys it. Follow her social media to connect, or email her directly at hello@taliahibbert.com.